The Mysterious Case
of the Missing Dog Walker

A Redemption Detective Agency Mystery

Books and series by Michele Pariza Wacek

Redemption Detective Agency
(Cozy Mysteries)
A spin-off from the Charlie Kingsley series.
https://MPWNovels.com/r/da_dwalker

Charlie Kingsley Mysteries
(Cozy Mysteries)
See all of Charlie's adventures here.
https://MPWnovels.com/r/ck_dwalker

Secrets of Redemption series
(Pychological Thrillers)
The flagship series that started it all.
https://MPWnovels.com/r/rd_dwalker

Mysteries of Redemption
(Psychological Thrillers)
A spin-off from the Secrets of Redemption series.
https://MPWnovels.com/r/mr_dwalker

Riverview Mysteries
(standalone Pychological Thrillers)
These stories take place in Riverview, which is near Redemption.
https://MPWnovels.com/r/rm_dwalker

The Mysterious Case of the Missing Dog Walker

A Redemption Detective Agency Mystery

by Michele Pariza Wacek

For my family, for always believing in me.

Chapter 1

"This is the most absurd thing I have ever done," I muttered to myself as I clomped up the stairs to the tidy blue and white ranch house. "And believe me, I know a lot about absurd things. Actually, probably too much."

It had only been a few weeks since I'd moved to Redemption, Wisconsin, to live with my Aunt Tilde and help her get her new business, The Redemption Detective Agency, off the ground. Never mind that my aunt was a retired nurse who knew absolutely nothing about solving cases. Nor did any of the other so-called "detectives" who also worked at the agency—Mildred, the retired schoolteacher, and Nora, the owner of a used bookstore in the same strip mall. Not to mention that none of them had any knowledge about running a business (including Nora, surprisingly enough, who technically DID own a business and really ought to know better).

But when you lose everything (and by "everything," I mean your job, your apartment, your car, your fiancé, AND your money), sometimes you find yourself doing completely unexpected things.

Like moving in with your aunt at thirty-one years old.

And searching for a dog that's been missing for over a year.

"A missing dog. Seriously?" I continued my muttering as I made my way across the carefully swept stoop to the dark-blue font door. Colorful pots filled with red, purple, and pink geraniums and a cheery pink and purple "Welcome" mat decorated the entrance. "Are these the types of cases The Redemption Detective Agency really wants to focus on?"

As soon as the words were out of my mouth, I wanted to drag them back in. I had a dreadful feeling that no, a missing dog would actually *not* be the most absurd case we would take on.

Likely not by a long shot.

How did this ever become my life? Just a few weeks before, I had a high-level job managing one of the top brokerage and investment firms in the state of Wisconsin. I was more or less running the place.

And now? I basically spent my days metaphorically herding cats while trying to manage what was *supposed* to be a business. Except it wasn't really a business. A business makes money, and that seemed to be the last thing anyone at The Redemption Detective Agency was interested in.

Which was how I found myself standing on a stranger's front stoop getting ready to open an investigation into a case involving a missing dog.

The dog's owner happened to be Trisha's aunt, and Trisha was our agency's attorney, Nick's, girlfriend. At least I assumed that was his official title, even though he wasn't getting paid. Not that it was any of my business. Nor was his relationship status. He was free to date whoever he pleased.

On second thought, maybe it should have been my business. Well, not the dating part. I didn't care about that … at all. Especially since I actually had my own someone to date. Jerome. In fact, I had a date with him that very night. So whatever Nick's relationship with Trisha was really didn't matter to me.

No, I was thinking about the money part—or, more specifically, the lack of money part. The more I contemplated it, the more I began to think that was probably the main reason Aunt Tilde wanted us to take the case. She probably thought helping out Nick's girlfriend's aunt would be a nice gesture … a way to pay him back for his time and energy, so to speak. Of course, she had given me a totally different reason.

"Think of the PR," she said as she straightened her orange-rimmed glasses, which perfectly matched her bright-orange hair. Neither matched her neon-orange blouse, though, which she had paired with a dark-green shawl to combat the temperature, thanks to the air conditioner being on the fritz and running way too cold. "Everyone loves a good dog story … especially one with a happy ending."

"What if it isn't a happy ending?" I asked sourly. Not that I wanted anything to happen to the dog, mind you. I truly hoped he was alive and well and living his best life in someone else's backyard. But the unfortunate reality was that tracking down a dog that's been missing for a year was highly unlikely. I also didn't particularly want anything to do with Trisha, her aunt, or her aunt's pet, but that was beside the point.

Aunt Tilde's eyes widened, and she put both her hands over Scout's ears. "Hush, don't say that so loud. You don't want to give him nightmares."

I rolled my eyes. Scout was my yellow lab mix, and even if he hadn't been currently sleeping on his pillow, I suspected my comment wouldn't have phased him. Despite her worry about his mental health, he seemed relatively unconcerned about the conversation. "I'm serious."

Aunt Tilde gave me a disapproving look. "So am I. You know about his past. There's no reason to remind him of it."

Scout was a stray who had been hanging out in my aunt's backyard until I took him in. "Oh, for Pete's sake. This isn't about Scout. It's about reality. You know as well as I do how difficult it is to find a lost dog after a few days, much less a year."

Aunt Tilde shook her head as she gave Scout an ear rub. He opened his eyes, lifted his head, and licked her face in return. "We can at least try. That's why our motto is 'Solving the unsolvable.'"

I winced, which is what I pretty much always did when I was reminded of our very unfortunate slogan. I was convinced it was a lawsuit waiting to happen. Aunt Tilde told me I was overthinking things again, and besides, if we DID solve the unsolvable, it would be a perfectly true claim.

Needless to say, that explanation didn't keep me from "overthinking."

"Just go talk to her," Aunt Tilde said before I could argue any more. "If you think it's really a lost cause, then fine. We can at least say we tried. But maybe you'll discover a clue she missed, and that clue will lead to us finding her dog."

That seemed completely preposterous for a whole bunch of reasons, but I could already tell by Aunt Tilde's set expression that anything I said would fall on deaf ears. Better for me to just agree and get it over with, as Aunt Tilde wasn't going to take "no" for an answer.

I just hoped my fear would prove unfounded, and it wouldn't be the total disaster I anxiously anticipated.

Regardless, I needed to do something other than stand there on her front porch fretting about all the ways the situation could go south. I took a deep breath of warm, geranium-scented summer air, squared my shoulders, and stepped toward the door. Might as well get it over with.

The neighborhood was eerily quiet, the sounds of cars, lawnmowers, even a child playing were completely non-existent. I wondered if the silence inside the house meant no one was home, and I couldn't decide if that would be good or bad. Good that I wouldn't have to have what I was sure would be a ridiculous conversation, but bad because it would mean I'd likely have to return and do the whole visit all over again. Ugh.

Well, enough stalling. I raised my hand and knocked briskly on the door.

Immediately, I was greeted with the sound of a dog yapping and toenails clicking across a tile floor. I frowned and took a step back, wondering if, after all my angst, I was at the wrong house. But before I could double-check the address, the door swung open.

"Can I help you?"

The woman standing in front of me looked like an older, flatter, less attractive version of Trisha. While Trisha was drop-dead gorgeous, with long, black, curly hair that reached halfway down her back, dark-blue eyes, and porcelain skin, this woman's wrinkles made her look tired, and her black-turning-silver hair was much shorter. Her dark-blue eyes, however, looked exactly the same as Trisha's. In her arms was a small, wriggling, snow-white dog who was trying very hard to free itself … probably so he could bite me. I'd never had much luck with other people's pets, or animals in general. Even the nicest ones, the ones whose owners swore would never hurt a fly, wanted to attack me. I found it was easier for everyone if I simply kept my distance.

Scout, of course, was the exception.

"Um." I eyed the dog, who I swore was staring at me like he knew how tasty I would be. In my experience, the smaller the dog, the more bloodthirsty they were. "Are you …" I suddenly realized

I didn't know the woman's name. Only that she was Trisha's aunt. Trisha had jotted down the address on the back of an electric bill and handed it to Aunt Tilde, and neither of them thought to add her aunt's name. Although I was hardly blameless, as it didn't occur to me to ask, either. Mentally, I kicked myself. What was I thinking? "Do you have a niece named Trisha?" I also realized I had no idea what Trisha's last name was. Why did I ever think I could be a detective? And, for that matter, what kind of detective agency sent its detectives out without providing the client's name?

I knew what kind—the kind that would end up getting sued over their ridiculous slogan, "Solving the unsolvable."

Ugh.

"I do." Her eyes widened. "Oh no. Did something happen to her?"

Oh geez. "No, no. I mean, she's fine," I quickly amended when I saw the look of horror spreading across her face. Man, this was not going well. "I'm here because she told me about your dog."

She looked surprised. "My dog? You mean little Rocky here?" She gently shook the dog, who seemed desperate to get down. I took a careful step back, wanting to be out of range of those little sharp teeth. "Are you thinking about getting a Maltese as well?"

"Ah, no. Your other dog."

Her face jerked up. "Other dog?"

It was like a door had slammed shut. Her entire manner instantly shifted. Her face went from cautiously friendly to completely shuttered. "Your other dog. The one who disappeared a year ago. She was wondering if we could … um …" I swallowed hard. "Maybe help look for him for you?" I sounded even more ridiculous than I had imagined, and her staring at me so warily wasn't helping.

If anything, her expression became even more stony. "I don't know what you're talking about. I didn't have a dog a year ago."

I blinked. Of all the ways I had imagined this conversation going, this was not one of them. "Um, but Trisha …"

"Trisha is wrong," she interrupted, her voice brusque. "This little guy is my dog. My *only* dog."

"Okay," I said, confused. I was starting to feel like I had stumbled into some sort of forbidden conversation topic, which made zero sense to me. I was asking about a missing dog. Why would that be so bad? "But why would Trisha think you had another dog?"

"Oh, who knows with Trisha," she snapped. Rocky, sensing the shift in her mood, stopped trying to wiggle away so he could attack me and instead started licking her face. It seemed to work, because her voice softened. "Oh, you're a good boy." She straightened up and started to step back into the house. "She probably got confused. Rocky did run away from me a few weeks ago. Scared me to death. The backyard gate was open, and I didn't realize it. It took me a couple of hours to find him, but he was fine. As you can see. Anyway, it was nice meeting you …"

"Emily," I said. "And you're …"

She didn't take the hint. Instead, she forced a smile on her face. "Emily. It's nice, Trisha having such good friends. Not everyone would help out someone's old aunt with a lost dog. But as you can see, everything is fine. Rocky is doing great." She gave him a big kiss as she backed into the house. "Thanks again for stopping by."

"Um, wait," I tried to say, but she was already closing the door, leaving me standing outside on her tidy stoop, surrounded by cheery geraniums and wondering what exactly had just happened.

Chapter 2

Other than the sound of Trisha's aunt's footsteps as she marched away from the door, the neighborhood was still silent. Did anyone else live there? What about the other animals, like the big fat squirrels I normally saw everywhere, or rabbits, or even birds; why weren't they around? I was starting to wonder if I had accidentally stepped inside an episode of *The Twilight Zone.* That would explain not only the puzzling conversation I just had with Trisha's aunt, but the lack of life surrounding me.

Slowly, I turned around, and as I did, a movement caught my eye. Next door, yellow curtains were fluttering near the window, like someone had been standing there, watching us.

Even if that is the case, so what, I tried to tell myself as the hairs at the back of my neck stood up. The thought was unsettling, even though there really was no reason for it. So Trisha's aunt had a nosey neighbor. Likely half of the houses in the country had nosey neighbors. It wasn't that uncommon.

Still.

As I stared at the window, I saw the curtains rustle again, and I realized the window was open. *Well, there you go,* I chided myself. *That's why the curtains were moving. The window is open. No one is watching. I was just being paranoid.*

But I still couldn't shake the feeling that something was off. The curtains had moved quite a bit, like someone had been standing there holding them open and then let them fall. Not to mention there was really no breeze to speak of.

And if someone *had* been standing there with the window open, that meant they could have been eavesdropping, as well. They could have heard every word of my conversation with Trisha's aunt …

I gave myself a quick shake and told myself to stop it. I was letting my imagination run away from me, and that wasn't like me.

I had been dawdling long enough. It was time to get back to the agency and let Aunt Tilde know this absurd case was officially over.

I strode down the driveway and back to my car, feeling like I should be pleased. I had more than enough to do. I certainly didn't need to waste time trying to track down a dog that had been missing for a year. This was a good thing.

But somehow, it didn't feel like it.

***

"Oh, a happy ending," Nora said, clasping her hands together. As usual, she was hanging out at The Redemption Detective Agency rather than her bookstore. She had long, dark-red, frizzy hair that always looked like it could use a good brushing, and her oversized glasses seemed to swallow her petite face. Her long, olive-green skirt hung on her too-thin frame, and her brown blouse was wrinkled. Her unpleasant gray cat Smoke skulked at her feet, giving Scout the side-eye. Before Scout became a regular visitor to The Redemption Detective Agency, Smoke used to terrorize Aunt Tilde's cat Sherlock, a little rescue calico, but Scout has since put Smoke in his place. "I'm so glad you were able to find Trisha's dog."

"Trisha doesn't have a dog," Mildred said. She was sitting at her neatly organized desk with her back straight. Her green pantsuit was carefully pressed, and her tight gray curls looked freshly permed.

"What are you talking about?" Nora asked, drawing her eyebrows together. "Emily just told us she found the dog."

Mildred peered at Nora over her glasses. "It wasn't Trisha who lost her dog. It was her cousin."

"Actually, it was her aunt," Aunt Tilde said. At least, that's what I thought she said. She was on her knees with a pencil clamped between her teeth as she flipped through one of the filing cabinets.

Mildred turned her head to peer at Aunt Tilde. "I'm pretty sure Trisha said it was her cousin."

"It was her aunt," I burst out, again wondering why conversations were so easily derailed at the agency. "But that's really not the point …"

"What do you mean, not the point?" Mildred was now peering at me. "I would think Trisha's cousin would want to be identified properly."

"I wouldn't know about Trisha's cousin because that's not who I visited," I said, trying to keep the exasperation out of my voice. "I talked to Trisha's aunt, and she told me she didn't have a dog that went missing."

Nora's brow furrowed. "I thought you said she had a dog."

"She does," I said, reminding myself to take deep breaths. Scout heaved himself off his bed and thrust his warm head into my hand while Smoke slunk further away. "It's a little white dog named Rocky."

"So the dog isn't missing, then. Right?" Nora asked. She still had a faintly puzzled expression on her face.

"Well, yes, but ..." Why did I feel like I was speaking a foreign language half the time? Scout pushed his head harder into my leg, and I rubbed his soft fur.

"So then, what's the problem? Case closed." Nora clapped her hands again.

"And good timing, because we have another one we need to get started on," Mildred said, moving her coffee cup over by an inch.

Another case? A real one, or another missing dog one? Did it include a paying client? All these questions and more swarmed on the tip of my tongue, but I bit them back before they could fly out of my mouth. I couldn't let them think that I had somehow "found" Trisha's aunt's dog. It wouldn't be right. "So hold on a minute. I still need to be clear. I didn't find Trisha's aunt's dog. She claims she never had a missing dog."

Mildred gave me "no kidding" look. "That's probably because you were talking to the wrong person. You should have been talking to Trisha's cousin."

"What? No, I told you, it was her aunt," I said, starting to feel flustered.

"How could it have been the aunt? You just said she didn't have a missing dog," Mildred said.

Emily, breathe deeply, I told myself again. "That's precisely my point. Trisha sent us there to help her aunt find her dog that went missing a year ago, and her aunt told me that Trisha was mistaken. That she never had a dog that went missing. Isn't that strange?"

"Maybe she forgot," Nora said.

Mildred gave her an odd look. "You think she forgot an entire dog?"

Nora shrugged. "It happens. I once forgot I had a boyfriend."

Mildred leaned across her desk. "You forgot … wait a minute. Was it that Stanley person?"

"There was nothing wrong with Stanley," Nora said defensively. "Mostly."

Mildred leaned back as she flapped her hands. "He was never your boyfriend. He was just a guy who would show up every now and then when he needed money."

"He did have his faults," Nora admitted.

"Well, I don't think it's the same thing. I can almost guarantee that a dog wasn't flitting in and out of her life, only showing up when he wanted a biscuit," Mildred said.

"I don't think she forgot she had a dog," I said. "Unless there's something more serious going on, like a medical issue. But that didn't seem to be the case."

Aunt Tilde popped her pencil out of her mouth. "So, let me get this straight. Are you saying that Trisha's aunt found her dog, so she doesn't need our help? Or that she never had a dog go missing?"

"That she never had a dog go missing," I said yet again, but at least this time, it seemed like someone was finally listening.

"But you also said she had a dog," Aunt Tilde said slowly.

"Yes, a little white dog."

Aunt Tilde sat back on her heels, her forehead wrinkling. "So maybe that was the dog Trisha was talking about, and Trisha just didn't realize the dog had been found."

Mildred sniffed. "Or *maybe* Trisha was talking about her cousin, not her aunt."

Aunt Tilde gave her a look. "Oh, for heaven's sake, she said aunt, not cousin."

"But don't you think-" I interrupted quickly, as I could see Mildred's mouth opening, and I wanted to derail another bickering session about aunt versus cousin. "Don't you think Trisha would have realized her aunt had a dog before now? This dog apparently went missing a year ago. Surely, she would have noticed if the dog was back before now."

"Unless they don't see each other very often," Aunt Tilde said. "That happens with families. They get busy or whatever. My guess is, she found the dog and just never told Trisha about it."

"You really think her aunt would make a point of telling her the dog was missing but not tell her it was found?" I asked.

"You don't know who told Trisha the dog was missing in the first place," Aunt Tilde said. "It may not have been her aunt, but someone else."

"And some families are terrible communicators," Nora piped in. "One of my friends found out her uncle died two years after his death."

Mildred stared at her. "Your friend didn't know her uncle died?"

"She wasn't particularly close to her family," Nora said.

"I would say not," Mildred said.

"So, you see, that's probably all this is. Just a communication error," Aunt Tilde said.

"I suppose," I said. I had to admit, what Aunt Tilde said made sense. At least logically. Who would lie about their dog not going missing? But I couldn't shake the uneasy feeling that there was still something off.

Well, it didn't matter. It wasn't like Trisha's aunt was going to be a paying customer, and if there was one thing The Redemption Detective Agency needed, it was more paying customers. Speaking of which …

"So why don't you tell us about this new case?" I asked.

Chapter 3

"We're going on a stakeout," Mildred announced happily. "Finally!" She said "finally" like The Redemption Detective Agency hadn't been on a stakeout for twenty years, despite it only having been open a couple of months.

"A stakeout. For what?" I asked.

Mildred's eyes narrowed. "For justice." She made a fist and hit the top of her desk, causing the coffee cup to jump and spill a few drops.

Justice? Oh, this sounded … not good. But before I could ask for clarification, Aunt Tilde was rising to her feet, her face flushed and eyes sparkling. In her hands was an overstuffed file, brimming with papers.

"Found it," she said triumphantly, waving the file. It looked dangerously close to losing some of its contents. "Emily, we're going to have to go shopping for all new equipment. I've got some marketing brochures right here to get you started."

"Equipment?" I asked suspiciously as Aunt Tilde handed me the file. "What kind of equipment?"

"Oh, you know." My aunt waved her hands airily. "Cameras, microphones, that sort of thing."

"We'll need some of those little ones that the government uses for bugging people's homes," Mildred said.

My jaw dropped. "Bugging? You want to bug someone's home?"

Mildred straightened up. "Whatever it takes. Justice must be done."

"But you can't just bug someone's house," I said. "I'm pretty sure that's illegal."

"Of course we can. We're licensed," Mildred said matter-of-factly.

"Being licensed doesn't mean you can do anything you want," I said, turning to Aunt Tilde and giving her a meaningful look. "Right?"

Aunt Tilde flapped her hands again. "Oh, Emily, of course we're not going to do anything bad. You should know better than that."

"I didn't say it was 'bad.' I said it was *illegal.*"

"Same difference," Aunt Tilde said.

"Besides, when you're in pursuit of justice, nothing is illegal," Mildred said.

I was fairly certain that also wasn't true, but clearly, I was losing the battle, so I decided to change the subject. "Exactly what kind of justice are we talking about?"

"Justice justice," Mildred said, shooting me a perplexed look. "What other kind is there?"

I took another deep breath. *Patience, Emily.* "I meant, what's the case about?"

"A cheating husband," Mildred said with a flourish. "And he's going to get his comeuppance, I assure you."

Well, at least that explained the stakeout and why we needed some decent cameras and lenses, but I was still going to put my foot down on the bugs. Speaking of bugs, I figured I'd better start looking through the file Aunt Tilde handed to me, to see what they thought was "essential" for a stakeout. Luckily, it seemed to be mostly advertisements and brochures for cameras, lenses and larger microphones. Some of them were pages torn out of a magazine.

"The wife is coming in for a meeting this afternoon." Aunt Tilde squinted at the clock. "Actually, she should be here in twenty minutes or so."

"Is this a paying client?" I held my breath as I continued flipping through the folder. Some of the camera prices were eye-popping.

"Of course," Aunt Tilde said with a sniff. "We are a business, after all. Not a hobby."

I glanced up in surprise. Maybe my lectures on how to run a business were getting through after all.

"Although I'm giving her a discount," Aunt Tilde continued, and just like that, my hopes were dashed.

"Why?"

She wrinkled her nose. "Well, it doesn't really fit our brand, you know. It's hardly an unsolvable case. Any detective agency could do it." Her voice held a hint of disdain, as if taking on paying clients to do routine detective work was something to be ashamed of. "But Mildred wanted to do a stakeout, so I thought it would be okay to make an exception."

"It wasn't just me," Mildred said, her voice huffy. "You wanted to go on one, too."

"Only if it fits the brand," Aunt Tilde insisted. "Managing a brand is very important. Isn't it, Emily?" She turned to me with an expectant look on her face, obviously waiting for me to agree with her. Except I was still stuck on the word "exception." Did she really mean that taking on a routine private investigation case with a paying customer was going to be the exception rather than the rule?

This business was never going to make any money, was it?

"Um, yes, brands are very important," I said carefully. Aunt Tilde smiled and shot Mildred an "I told you so" look. "But," I continued, "just because you have a business brand doesn't mean you can't take on other types of cases. Especially cases that are … typical and common in our industry."

I expected some pushback, but Aunt Tilde beamed at me. "Emily, you always know the right thing to say. I didn't want to admit it, but I was a little worried making this exception would hurt our brand. It's good to know we can take on a case like this from time to time."

"What? No, that's not what I meant," I started to say, but Aunt Tilde had moved on and was pointing to the file in my hand. "Another plus is finally having a good reason to get this equipment."

I looked down at the stuffed folder again. There seemed to be hundreds of flyers. My heart sank. It was going to take some time to research and figure out which items would be best, and I had a feeling time wasn't something I was going to have a lot of.

"And don't skimp," Mildred said, shaking her finger at me. "We're going to need the good stuff. The last thing we want is for the something to break down right when we need it."

"I'll do my best," I said, staring at the folder and wondering if I should bring it home with me so I could start going through it. Oh, no, I couldn't. I had a date.

"A stakeout," Nora said, clapping her hands. "I'm so excited. I'll bake cookies to bring." She frowned. "Maybe I should create a list, so we don't all bring the same thing. You know, like they do for potlucks."

Before anyone could tell her this wasn't a party, but work (although, on second thought, maybe I was alone in that thought, and the other two were going to volunteer to bring food items, too), the little bell above the door jingled, and in walked Nick.

For a moment, my heart seemed to stop in my chest. As usual, he was a little rumpled, with his pale-green shirt unbuttoned at the neck, his tie loosened, and sleeves rolled up. His black hair was a little messy, and he sported his normal five o'clock shadow. Even though I reminded myself that I preferred men who were more put together, generally speaking, with pressed shirts and neat haircuts, my body didn't seem to be listening.

He paused in the doorway, his expression almost uncertain as his dark-green eyes scanned the room. Flashing us a crooked grin, he said, "Sorry, didn't mean to interrupt."

"Don't be silly. You could never interrupt us," Aunt Tilde said as Scout stood up from his pillow, stretched, and padded over to greet him. Nick rubbed his neck as Scout leaned against him, his tongue lolling out. It was all I could do to not scowl at Scout. Traitor.

"Is there something you need from us?" Aunt Tilde continued.

"Nope. I just wanted to stop by and check something out in the kitchen." The kitchen was an actual commercial kitchen, as the space we were occupying used to be for restaurants. Or, more accurately, for failed restaurants. When we moved in, not only was the kitchen filthy, but it was home to an entire civilization of cockroaches. Needless to say, that was one of the first things I took care of when I started working at The Redemption Detective Agency.

However, a detective agency didn't have much use for a commercial kitchen (even a clean and cockroach-free one), so Nick was remodeling it into something more useful for us. He was also donating his time and labor, which was nice, since we currently didn't have any paying clients. Scratch that—very shortly, we would have one … although it appeared any earnings from that case were going straight toward purchasing cameras and microphones.

However, Nick helping around the office also meant I couldn't avoid seeing him.

As if he were reading my mind, he turned and pinned those dark-green eyes on me. "Hi, Emily. I didn't see you there." There was something about the way he said my name that felt like a caress, and I shivered despite myself.

"You shouldn't bother Emily. She has a lot to do, especially since she has plans tonight," Mildred said, a pointed edge to her voice. Nick's eyes flashed with some unidentifiable emotion, but before I could pinpoint it, he had tucked it away again, his expression smooth and unruffled.

For some reason, that infuriated me. What right did he have to be upset by my dating life? He was the one dating Trisha, for heaven's sake. Not that it was any of my business.

I straightened my shoulders and lifted my chin. "Hi, Nick. We appreciate you stopping by, especially on a Friday night … I'm sure you have plans, as well."

He stood up, his eyes shuttered. "As a matter of fact, I do. I won't be too long." He gave Scout one last pat before heading toward the kitchen, his long legs striding across the floor while I tried not to look at how nicely he filled out his gray dress pants.

I glanced away only to notice Mildred eyeing me, her expression faintly disapproving. She opened her mouth to say something, which I was sure I didn't want to hear, when the door tinkled again.

"Nick, hurry up." A high, whiney voice drifted into the agency, the sound like nails on a chalkboard. "We don't want to be late for our reservations- oh …" Trisha stepped into the room and surveyed it. "I'm looking for Nick." Like that wasn't apparent.

In the corner of my eye, I saw Mildred purse her lips disapprovingly, but Aunt Tilde flashed her a warm smile. "He's in the kitchen."

Trisha huffed a sigh, jutting out a hip and removing her sunglasses. "I'm not going in there unless I have to. I don't want to mess up my outfit." She gestured toward her little black miniskirt, and I couldn't help but notice her tight, red, low-cut blouse that displayed her ample wares. Her long, jet-black hair was pulled into a complicated updo, with a few tendrils framing her beautiful, heavily made-up face.

Even though I didn't want to, I found myself comparing myself to her. Me, with my brownish-blondish hair pulled back into a simple ponytail, my only makeup a dash of mascara to highlight my blue-gray eyes and a smudge of pink lipstick that I was sure was faded out by now, and respectful (but plain) dark-blue short-sleeved polo shirt and white shorts that started the day pressed, but had since wilted in the heat.

Ugh, I hated her.

But I also quickly swallowed that hatred. Right now, she was the only lead I had, in terms of sorting out the odd conversation I'd had with her aunt.

So, I plastered a smile on my face. "Trisha, I'm so glad you stopped by."

Trisha was preoccupied with the small mirror she had dug out of her purse to examine her makeup. "Hmm?"

Ugh. Why did I even bother? Her aunt clearly didn't want my help, and it wasn't like I didn't just have a giant project dumped into my lap. Nevertheless, a part of me (a small but mighty part) doggedly plowed on. "I went to see your aunt today."

That got a reaction. She snapped her mirror shut and turned toward me. "Aunt Gin? Oh, wonderful! How is she doing?"

Well, if nothing else, I at least had a first name now. "She seems great," I said cautiously. "I also met her dog."

"Oh, yes. Rocky. He's a cutie, isn't he? She just got him a few months ago." She glanced over at Scout, who had settled back onto his dog bed, and then at Sherlock, who was sleeping on her cat tower. "You have such a cute dog, as well. What's his name again?"

"Scout," I said.

She leaned forward. "Scout! What a sweet doggie you are."

Scout lifted one eyelid, stared at her, and shut it again.

Trisha stood up, putting her hands on her hips and pouting. "Oh. Why doesn't he come see me?"

"Well, he's a rescue, so you know," I said, waving my hands and trying to sound sympathetic even though inside, I was gleefully promising Scout an extra-special treat for dinner. I might even forgive him for betraying me with Nick. "Anyway, I thought you said your aunt's dog had run away a year ago."

"Her *cousin's* dog," Mildred corrected me.

Trisha looked at her in confusion. "What?"

"She meant your cousin's dog," Mildred said.

Trisha looked even more perplexed. "My cousin? You mean Bonny?"

"Yes, Bonny," Mildred said, nodding knowingly. Like she knew anything. It was all I could do not to roll my eyes.

Trisha now looked mystified. "That's strange. I didn't even realize she had a dog."

"Well, how could she? The dog ran away a year ago. Right?" Mildred asked.

Trisha frowned as she slowly nodded. "Yeeesss …"

"Anyway," I finally was able to interject, taking a couple of steps closer to Trisha in hopes that Mildred would take the hint and let me finish the conversation before Nick whisked her off to their amazing romantic evening. "As I was saying … I saw your aunt today."

Trisha turned to me, a faint furrow between her eyes. "Are you talking about my Aunt Gin or my cousin Bonny?"

"Your Aunt Gin. And Rocky," I added, as it suddenly occurred to me Trisha may have a second aunt lurking around.

Her face cleared. "Yes, he's a sweetie, isn't he?"

I pictured his squirming body, desperate to get down, and those tiny pointy teeth, and nodded. "Yes, he's very sweet. Was Rocky the dog you were talking about who had gone missing? Or was it another dog?"

Her forehead once again puckered in confusion. "Rocky didn't go missing. Well, I think he got away from Aunt Gin once or twice, but he's a puppy. That's what puppies do. No, Rex was the one who went missing."

My heart quickened in my chest. "Rex?"

"Yeah, he was a German shepherd. Just a sweetheart. You wouldn't think he would be … I know some people think that breed is mean. But he didn't have a mean bone in his body."

"A German shepherd," I said faintly. There was no way anyone would mistake a German shepherd with that little ball of white fluff and sharp teeth. "And …Rex, did you say? He went missing a year ago?"

Trisha nodded. "Yeah. Aunt Gin must have been frantic. She loved that dog to pieces. I was so glad she got Rocky, so at least she has another one around to keep her company."

"Sounds like she needed one then," I said, trying to keep my voice casual. "Can you think of any reason why she would tell me she didn't have another dog?"

Trisha was staring at me like I had lost my mind. "What are you talking about? Of course she has a dog. You just told me you met Rocky."

"Not Rocky. Rex."

"I don't understand. She told you she didn't own Rex?"

"She didn't tell me Rex's name, but yes. That she never had another dog."

Trisha looked floored. "Why would she deny owning Rex? That makes no sense."

"I know. That's why I was hoping you might be able to shed some light on it."

She pursed her lips, shifting her stance by sticking one hip out and folding her arms across her chest. "You must have misunderstood her," she finally announced. "Or she misunderstood you."

"No, I'm pretty sure we understood each other."

She shook her head firmly. "No. There was some sort of miscommunication going on. That's the only explanation." There was a note of finality to her voice, and she went back to examining her reflection in her compact.

I nodded, even though she wasn't looking at me anymore. "Okay, well maybe that is what happened. Do you mind talking to her about it? Because if she …" I had to swallow hard to push the next words out. "If she did lose Rex, we would love to be able to find him for her."

She gave me a hard look. "What do you mean, 'if?' I told you, Rex went missing a year ago."

I put my hands up. "Okay, okay. We'd love to help your aunt Gin, if we could. So, would you mind talking to her?"

"Oh, Trisha. I didn't know you were here." Nick had come out of the kitchen and was standing behind us, a wary expression on his face as his eyes shifted between us. "I would have picked you up."

"That's okay. I wanted to surprise you, and your secretary told me you were here," Trisha said, but her voice lacked her usual flirtation, and there was a still a furrow between her eyes. Then, she turned back to me. "I'll talk to her," she said.

Nick looked slightly alarmed. "Talk to who?"

Trisha stepped closer to him, slipping her hand into the crook of his arm. "My aunt Gin."

That didn't seem to pacify him. "Your aunt Gin? What do you need to talk to her about?"

"I'll tell you in the car," she said, nudging him toward the door. Nick allowed himself to be led, albeit reluctantly.

"You know," Mildred said to me, "none of this would have happened if you had just gone to see Bonny."

"Actually, Mildred," I said as I made my way back to my desk, "you're absolutely right."

Chapter 4

I had barely opened the folder of brochures when the bell above the door jingled yet again, and a woman entered the office. She wore a shapeless beige blouse with loose-fitting navy shorts. Her brown eyes peered out owlishly from behind gold-rimmed glasses perched on a face scrubbed clean of makeup. Her brown hair was scraped back into a tight bun. I wouldn't necessarily call her ugly, but she was certainly … plain. A little makeup, a brighter blouse, and a more flattering hairstyle would have made a massive difference.

She hovered near the door with uncertainty, as if one wrong move might compel her to bolt. It was like watching a hungry mouse trying to decide if it should scurry across the floor and risk being eaten by one of the cats or slink back into its hole in the wall and suffer. I was thinking the hole in the wall was about to win out when Aunt Tilde jumped in.

"You must be Jan," Aunt Tilde greeted her with a big smile as she got to her feet. Ah. The new client.

Jan responded with a slight nod, looking only marginally less terrified. She was clutching her brown purse to her chest so tightly, it was as if she were afraid someone was about to snatch it from her.

"I'm so glad you made it," Aunt Tilde said as Scout got up from his bed again, gave himself a quick shake, and moseyed over to her. "That's Scout. He's friendly," Aunt Tilde said as I jumped up, ready to rescue our mouse-like client from Scout, should he get too excited, but unlike the rest of us, Scout didn't seem to faze her. She gave Scout a scratch behind the ears as Aunt Tilde introduced the rest of us.

"Come, sit over here, and tell us how we can help you," Mildred said, gesturing to the empty space in front of her desk. "Can I get you some coffee?"

"Sure," Jan said, her voice faint and her brow furrowed as she searched the room for an empty chair. I quickly dragged mine to the empty space and gestured for her to take a seat, making a mental note to buy another chair or two along with the stakeout equipment.

Jan sank down in the chair as Mildred fetched her some coffee, and Aunt Tilde settled herself behind her desk with a notebook open and pen ready. Nora scooted her chair closer, managing to run over the Smoke's tail, who let out a yowl. In response, Mildred spilled the coffee all over the counter, and Jan nearly fell out of her chair.

"Sorry," Nora said, clearly self-conscious as she bent over to comfort a highly offended Smoke.

"So all of you are detectives here?" Jan asked, gesturing weakly with one hand.

"We are," Aunt Tilde answered proudly, sitting straighter in her chair. "But we also have different roles, as well. Like Emily there," she nodded to me. "She's also our office manager."

Jan turned to look at me as I gave her a self-conscious wave. She pressed her lips together into a semblance of a smile and turned back to Aunt Tilde. "I have to say, this is a much bigger operation than I was expecting," Her tone didn't make it sound like a good thing. Would she prefer a one-man agency, I wondered? She continued talking as she accepted the new cup of coffee from Mildred. "But Greta said so many good things about you, I knew just you were the right one."

Aunt Tilde's chest puffed up. "Greta is such a dear. I'm just grateful we were able to set that wrong right. It's so sweet of her to pass our name around. Our phones have been ringing off the hook." That was news to me. Other than the phone company trying to entice us into buying advertising space in the upcoming yellow pages phonebook and a couple of wrong numbers, the phone hadn't rung much at all. "But how can we help you?" Aunt Tilde asked, an innocent, butter-wouldn't-melt-in-my-mouth expression on her face.

Jan stared at her hands, one clutching her purse and the other her untouched coffee. "Well, like I said on the phone, I'm afraid my husband is cheating on me."

"That jerk," Mildred said immediately, shaking her head and clucking her tongue. "Men. Can't live with them, can't shoot 'em."

Jan reared her head up, a startled expression on her face. "But I don't want to shoot him."

"Of course not," Aunt Tilde rushed in, flashing Mildred a hard look. "It's just a saying."

Mildred frowned and muttered something under her breath.

"Anyway, go on," Aunt Tilde said.

Jan gave Mildred another uneasy look before turning her attention to her purse again. "It's just, if he is cheating on me, I'm worried he might leave me." Her voice broke with the words "leave me."

"Oh, I'm sure he wouldn't," Nora said. "Just because he's cheating on you doesn't mean he wants to leave you. He's probably just …" here, she fluttered one of her hands, "sowing his oats. Men do that, you know. But it doesn't mean he's going to leave you."

"Well, I say better safe than sorry," Mildred said briskly. "You never know what men will do. It's good you're here, protecting yourself and finding out the truth."

One of Jan's fists started squeezing the purse strap, turning the skin white.

"Nora is right," Aunt Tilde said gently, having noticed what Jan was doing to her purse, too. "Mildred is right, as well. You absolutely should protect yourself. But just because he's cheating doesn't necessarily mean he wants to leave you."

"But he might," Jan burst out almost uncontrollably, as if the words had been waiting for that exact moment to break free. "And if he does, I'll have nothing."

"Of course you'll have something," Mildred said in her firm, no-nonsense, teacher voice. "You'll have your self-respect."

I tried not to roll my eyes.

Jan stared at her, her expression close to hysterical. "But I won't have any money!"

"Oh, I'm sure that wouldn't be the case," Mildred said. "You'd get something in the divorce settlement."

But Jan was violently shaking her head. "No, you don't understand. He's the one with all the money and connections. I don't have any of that. If he divorces me, and I can't prove he was cheating, I'll have nothing."

"Then we'll just have to make sure we catch him," Mildred said with a gleam in her eye. "He won't get away with it."

Jan pressed a hand against her chest, as if trying to physically slow her heavy, labored breathing. The coffee had sloshed over in her other hand and was dripping onto the floor, but she seemed not to notice. "You really think you can do that?"

"Of course!" Mildred said, like she couldn't even believe Jan was questioning her. "We have a nearly 100% success rate!"

With only one case, I thought, trying again not to roll my eyes.

"You're in very capable hands," Aunt Tilde said warmly. "We'll take very good care of you."

Jan took a deep breath and gave Aunt Tilde and Mildred a weak smile. "Thank you. You've made me feel so much better about everything already."

"That's what we're here for," Aunt Tilde said. "We can get started right away. Does that work for you?"

"Sure," Jan said, her expression a little mystified. "But don't you want me to sign a contract and pay the deposit first?"

"That won't be necessary," Aunt Tilde said at the exact same time I said, "Yes, that would be perfect." I pulled a blank contract out of the bottom drawer of my desk, which I had turned into a mini filling cabinet. Clipping the contract to a clipboard, I noticed Aunt Tilde's eyes light up. "Oh, Emily. I should have known you would think of everything." She leaned closer to Jan, as if telling her a secret. "She had a job managing one of the biggest Duckworth companies in Riverview. We are so lucky to have snatched her up."

I glared at Aunt Tilde, willing her with my eyes to keep her mouth shut while struggling to maintain a pleasant smile on my face. Ugh. She knew better than to bring up my former job at Duckworth Brokerage and Investments. Even though I was the one who had uncovered an embezzlement operation, they had still fired me. Actually, it was more than just a simple firing. They had blackballed me, so no one would hire me. Apparently, that's what happens when you uncover something that could embarrass the most powerful family in Wisconsin. It's not the family member doing the embarrassing thing (in this case, the embezzling) who is punished—oh no, it's the one who figured it out who has her life ruined.

Or would have been ruined if it hadn't been for my Aunt Tilde.

As grateful as I continued to be for her help, she really, really needed to keep her mouth shut. Even though we were in Redemption, which was forty-five minutes away from Riverview, it wasn't nearly far enough away from the Duckworths' influence. I was still hurting over the loss of my best friend Deena, who was forced to distance herself from me because of her boyfriend and his career. It made me wonder how many lives had been destroyed because they had gotten on the wrong side of the Duckworths.

Jan's eyes were as round as saucers. "You worked for the Duckworths?"

"In a past life," I said lightly, trying to ignore my stomach tightening. I handed her the contract and a pen. "If you can fill this out and sign …"

She took the items from me, balancing the clipboard on her lap so she could still clutch her untouched coffee, her eyes never leaving mine. "What are they like?"

Like? She wanted to know what the Duckworths were like? Bile rose up in the back of my throat, but I forced it down. "They were fine. I didn't actually know them very well. Now, here's where you fill out your name and address." I tapped the contract.

She obediently positioned her pen where I had gestured, but she was still staring at me. "I would have loved to have had your job and gotten to know that family. My mother used to subscribe to *The Riverview Times*, and when I was a little girl, we used to read the gossip column together. It sounded like they led such a glamorous life." She sighed dramatically.

Seriously? I wanted to throttle Aunt Tilde so badly, my hands itched. "Truly, it wasn't that exciting," I said. "They're basically just like you and me. You know, putting their pants on one leg at a time." I smiled, trying to make a joke out of it, but Jan's expression turned horrified.

"How can you say that?" Jan practically gasped. "They're nothing like us!"

I took a step back, a little uncomfortable with her intensity. "Um … well …"

"I met one of the Duckworths once," Nora said suddenly. "They came into my bookstore."

Jan's head jerked around. "You met one of them? In Redemption?"

Nora shrugged. "They come by from time to time. I think they like to check out how the other half lives." She let out a little laugh.

I was finding it difficult to believe that any Duckworth would set foot in a used bookstore, much less a used bookstore located in a strip mall with a pawn store and a dry cleaner, but Jan had no such misgivings. "What did they buy?"

Nora screwed up her face. "Let's see. He bought a Tom Clancy book. I'm pretty sure it was Tom Clancy. And she bought a couple of Danielle Steel romances." She frowned. "I think he might have been flirting with me, too."

Okay, so there was no way that happened. Whoever walked into her shop was no Duckworth.

Mildred seemed to have the same thought as she stared at Nora, her mouth pressed into a straight line. "You're trying to tell us one of the Duckworths was flirting with *you*?"

"Why not?" Nora said defensively before pursing her lips. "Although now that I think about it, it was sort of weird, as he had a woman with him."

"Maybe that's because he wasn't flirting with you," Mildred said.

Nora frowned. "No, I think he was. I'm pretty sure." She started nodding. "Yes, yes. The more I think about it, the surer I am. Although …" her voice trailed off, and her brow furrowed. "Was his name Duckworth, or Dunkin?"

Jan gave Nora a hard look before turning back to me. "Are you still in touch with the family?"

I took a step back. There was something almost … hungry, in her gaze. Almost like she wanted to eat me. "Um, no. Not really."

Her face fell. "That's too bad."

"Well, it's what happens when you leave a job," I said, still trying to keep my voice light.

"So, maybe you should tell us more about your husband," Aunt Tilde suggested.

Ugh. While I appreciated my aunt trying to change the subject, did we really want her as a client? I sure didn't. But a quick peek at the anticipation on Mildred's face made me realize I was in the minority. "Before you do, you really ought to sign the contract," I said.

Jan eyed me, an unreadable expression on her face, before grasping the pen and quickly filling out the form. She handed it back to me without another word.

Aunt Tilde cleared her throat. "So, now …"

"Deposit too," I interrupted. With any luck, she would balk at paying this minute, which might give me some time to try to talk the rest of them out of taking her case. But no. Jan whipped a checkbook out of her purse, promptly filled out the check, and handed it to me. "Are we good?" she asked. "Or do you need to deposit it first?"

"No, no, this is fine," I said, retreating to my desk. Aunt Tilde's expression was nothing short of delighted, and I was a little worried about what she might say. But Jan was already talking as she pulled a huge file out of her purse, telling us how she had compiled everything we might need to find out if her husband was cheating on her.

I tucked the contract and check into my desk drawer, then turned my attention to my notes, hoping we weren't making a big mistake.

Chapter 5

"I can't believe you haven't been here yet," Jerome said, picking up his beer. "The Tipsy Cow is practically a landmark here in Redemption."

After a very nice dinner at Mario's, an upscale Italian restaurant, Jerome invited me to have an after-dinner drink with him at The Tipsy Cow. Even though I had already enjoyed two glasses of wine with dinner, which is normally my limit, I figured one more drink wouldn't hurt. It was a Friday night, after all, and while I did have to start researching equipment this weekend (as it was all I could do to keep Mildred from calling the manufacturers herself once Jan left), I could certainly sleep in on a Saturday morning first.

Jerome was a true gentleman. He picked me up right on time, wearing a pressed button-down shirt and tie. He didn't just talk about himself, but asked me questions as well, and was interested in what I had to say. He was sweet and charming, and the more time I spent with him, the more relaxed I was and the more I enjoyed myself. In fact, we talked so much that we basically closed the place down, so when Jerome offered to continue the conversation at The Tipsy Cow, it was an easy yes.

Maybe Mildred was better at this matchmaking thing than I gave her credit for.

"Well, I haven't been in Redemption very long," I said, spinning my wine glass as I looked around. There was a big crowd, but the bar was a decent size, so there were still tables available near the back, which was where we were. It was full of polished wood, from the floor to the walls to tables, and smelled of cigarette smoke, beer, and perfume. There was also a trace of fried food in the air, and Jerome told me they also served lunch and dinner.

He was looking at me intently. "Do you think you're going to stay?" As soon as the words were out of his mouth, his cheeks turned red, and he gave me an abashed look. "Sorry. That came out a little more forcefully than I intended."

I smiled at him, mostly to set him at ease. "It's okay. I don't really know how long I'm going to be here, but I don't see myself leaving for a while." *If ever,* I thought, but I didn't say it. Truth be told, I sometimes despaired I would be spending the rest of my life living above my aunt's garage and working in her more-hobby-than-business business—also known as The Redemption Detective Agency. If the agency never made any money, I didn't see how I was ever going to save enough to be able to move out. As for finding a different job, that was going to be tough, as well, as no one wanted to cross the Duckworths … at least the ones who had positions I was qualified for and that would pay enough for me to live on my own. So, at least for now, I was stuck where I was. Maybe, hopefully, in a few years, things would be different.

But I didn't want to tell Jerome all of that. He didn't need to know my sob story, especially on a first date. I squelched the little voice inside me that reminded me I had poured my heart out to Nick, and not even on a date!, but that didn't count. With Nick, it was just right place, right time. Or maybe I should say wrong place, wrong time, as now he knew far more about my past than he should.

Enough of Nick. I was on a lovely date with Jerome, just like Nick was with Trisha.

"Do you like working as a PI?"

"Oh, I'm not a private investigator," I said quickly, stopping myself from adding, *I don't think there's anyone at The Redemption Detective Agency who could be considered a PI.* "I'm the office manager."

"That's right, you said that." He hit himself lightly on the side of his head, making a face as he did. "Although it does sound like you do some investigating work."

"Aunt Tilde has an … open-door policy when it comes to the detectives," I said. "Basically, we can all jump in and help solve the cases. Which I appreciate, but really, I'm more comfortable in my office manager role."

"How do you like working with your aunt?" He lowered his voice, as if we were sitting in the agency and Aunt Tilde was in the next room, rather than a very noisy bar on a Friday night. "Is it stressful working with family?"

"Absolutely," I said, thinking about how Aunt Tilde had let my employment history with the Duckworths slip out to Jan, not to mention a million other things she did that rubbed me the wrong way. Or how running The Redemption Detective Agency in a professional manner always felt like an uphill battle.

But, on the other hand, I was the only person there to get paid. And she also gave me complete freedom to manage the agency any way I saw fit, even if half the time, no one could remember the procedures I put in place. "Although it's not ... *Aunt Tilde?*"

"Wait, what did you say?" Jerome asked, looking around confusedly as Aunt Tilde waved at me from across the bar.

It couldn't really be her. There was no way my aunt would be at a bar late on a Friday night. I had to be hallucinating. Could wine make you hallucinate? I seemed to recall that it could, but surely, two or three glasses wouldn't trigger a hallucination. Would it?

Maybe I had passed out and was dreaming. That made more sense.

I gave my head a quick shake, hoping to jerk myself awake. No, she was still there, a big smile lighting up her face. I squeezed my eyes shut and opened them again. For a moment, I couldn't find her, and my heart leaped ... but then I realized it was only because another woman had stepped between us, blocking my view.

"It's ... uh ... my Aunt Tilde," I said as my arm slowly raised up, as if on its own accord, to return her wave.

Jerome blinked at me. "Your ... *Aunt Tilde* is here?"

The woman between my aunt and me spun around, and my stomach hit the ground.

"And Mildred," I added faintly as Mildred's eyes lit up. Without even a moment of hesitation, she marched determinedly toward our table.

Jerome's jaw dropped. "*Mildred* is here?"

"Well, hello you two," Mildred sang out. "Fancy meeting you here." She had changed her outfit and was now wearing a cream, silk blouse with several strands of necklaces. Aunt Tilde, who was right behind her, had also dressed up for the occasion in a bright-pink top and leopard-print jacket.

"Um, yes," I said, still trying to process that Aunt Tilde and Mildred had shown up *on my date*. It had to be a bad dream. "What *are* you doing here?"

"Oh, Tilde and I thought we'd grab a drink, right Tilde?" Mildred asked, waving toward Aunt Tilde as she continued to study us, her eyes gleaming. "How are you two getting along?"

I refused to let her change the subject. "You just thought, out of the blue, that you would have a drink at The Tipsy Cow?"

Mildred's eyes narrowed at me. "It's Friday night, after all. Why can't we have a drink?"

Aunt Tilde elbowed Mildred in the ribs. "Yes, let's go have that drink and leave the young ones alone. They get enough of us during the week. I'm sure they could both use a little break."

You have no idea, I thought, but didn't say, as much as I wanted to. Instead, I plastered a fake smile on my face. "There's a table open over there," I said, pointing across the bar.

Mildred glanced in that direction and made a face. "Nonsense. There's a perfectly good table right there." "Right there" was about five feet away from us. It was all I could to not jump up and drag Jerome to the table I was pointing to.

Aunt Tilde began pushing Mildred toward the table nearby. "Now, don't mind us," she was saying. "We're just here for a quick drink. You won't even know we're here."

"Yeah, I'll believe that when it happens," I muttered, dropping my forehead into my hand. But then, a thought occurred to me, and I snapped my head up. "Wait, how did you know we would be here?"

They both stared at me, eyes wide and "cat that ate the canary" expressions on their faces. "Oh … I don't know," Mildred said, waving her hands as Aunt Tilde added, "Lucky guess!"

Lucky guess, my foot.

Both of them made a big deal of getting settled into their seats. I tried to ignore them, purposefully focusing on my wine instead, draining most of it in a single swallow. "Sorry about that," I said to Jerome, who was looking at me oddly. Great. Apparently, this was going to be our first and last date. Ugh. I was really starting to like this guy, too. *Thanks, Mildred.*

Jerome cleared his throat, and I braced myself, waiting for him to tell me how he actually *did* need to leave, as he just remembered something urgent he had to do in the morning … like sort his sock drawer. Instead, he gave me a sheepish look. "I think I'm the one who owes you an apology."

I looked at him in surprise. "Why?"

A faint blush appeared high on his cheeks. "Because I'm the one who told Mildred what we were doing tonight."

My jaw dropped. "You did?"

He nodded grimly before taking a long swallow of beer. "She found me earlier in the day and asked what my plans were. I didn't see the harm in it. Plus, I thought maybe she could give me a heads up if you'd object to what I was planning. So, I told her." He winced and lowered his voice. "I never thought she'd actually *show up*."

"It's not your fault," I said. "I mean, why *would* you think that?" I cocked my head to study him. "You really wanted to make sure I wouldn't have a problem with what you planned for tonight?"

He shifted uncomfortably in his chair. "Of course. I wanted to make a good impression." His expression turned bashful and a little unsure. "Is that okay?"

I felt a surge of warmth in my chest. Jerome wanted to make a good impression on me. I couldn't remember the last time a man wanted to do that. Certainly not Geoff, my former fiancé. I couldn't recall him ever trying to impress me, even when we were first dating. "Absolutely."

He grinned at me, and my heart fluttered. He really was good looking, especially when he smiled.

There was a tap on my shoulder. "Did Jerome tell you that he's the youngest principal the school has ever had?" Mildred practically shouted in my ear, probably because it was so noisy. I winced and tried to lean away.

I glanced at Jerome and saw the tips of his ears had turned red. I thought it was adorable. "Um, no, it didn't really come up."

"Oh, he's too modest," Mildred said, her voice fond. "He's a wonderful principal, and I should know. You wouldn't believe what I had to put up with over the years. My word."

"I can imagine," I said faintly.

"Oh, here comes the waitress," Jerome said, waving frantically. "Have you decided on what you're going to order?"

"I have," Aunt Tilde said. "I'm going to have a Pink Lady. I haven't had one in ages. What about you, Mildred?"

"Oooh, that sounds good. Maybe I'll have one too," Mildred said before turning back to us, clearly not taking Jerome's hint. "What about you, Emily?"

"I'm drinking wine," I said, dangling my nearly empty glass to show her before finishing it.

She laughed. "Oh, you're so funny. Jerome, did you notice how funny she is?"

"I did," Jerome said, his voice deadpan.

"Of course I didn't mean what you were drinking," she continued, as I tried to unobtrusively determine whether there was enough room for me to hide under the table. "I wanted to know if you've told Jerome how helpful you've been at The Redemption Detective Agency?"

"Mildred!" I was horrified and could feel my own ears burning. "That's not something that would come up in conversation."

"Well, it should," Mildred said determinedly as she patted my arm. "She's been absolutely wonderful. We couldn't do it without her."

"I'm sure," Jerome said, a slight smile on his face. I, however, was about ten seconds away from *diving* under the table—or maybe into a bottle of wine would be better. I looked longingly at my empty glass.

"Mildred, should we get an appetizer?" Aunt Tilde yelled. "I'm thinking about getting some fried cheese curds. Or maybe the fried platter that has a little of everything … fried mushrooms, zucchini, and onion rings, along with the cheese curds."

"Oh, that's a wonderful idea," Mildred said. "Then we'll have enough to share." She gave us a hopeful look, and I wondered what had happened to "you won't even know we're here."

"I don't think the kitchen is open," I said.

"You want chicken wings?" Aunt Tilde asked, peering at the little sign holder that was perched on each table listing the daily special.

"Oh, you don't want chicken wings on a date," Mildred said, clucking her tongue. "Way too messy."

"That's true, they are messy," Aunt Tilde said. "The combo platter would be better."

"I didn't say chicken wings," I said more loudly. "I said I don't think the kitchen is open."

Aunt Tilde furrowed her brow. "Why wouldn't it be? The bar is open."

"Yes, but the bar and kitchen are separate," I said.

"That doesn't make sense," Mildred said, returning to her seat and taking the little sign from Aunt Tilde. "If you're open, your kitchen should be open. Besides, why would they have this here, if we couldn't order food?"

"Because it's too much work to remove it every night," I said.

"Well, that's terrible customer service," Mildred said, glaring at the little sign like it was its fault it was still on the table. "How are people supposed to know they can't order food then?"

"The hours the kitchen is open are probably on there," I said.

Mildred squinted at it. "Heavens … how can anyone read all that little text?"

"Here, let me see it," Aunt Tilde said, reaching for it, but Mildred didn't let her have it.

"Oh, your eyesight isn't any better than mine," Mildred said.

I sighed and rubbed my forehead, wondering if I should offer to read the sign for them, or if that would just compound the problem.

"Here," Jerome said. He had picked up the little sign on our table and was reading it, and a part of me wanted to hit myself in the head. Of course there would be one on our table, too. "Unfortunately, Emily is right. The kitchen service ended an hour ago." He flashed me a conspiratorial grin, and I felt my chest grow warm.

Mildred's face fell. "Oh, that's disappointing. I would have loved some cheese curds."

Aunt Tilde looked equally distraught. "Late-night munchies would have hit the spot. Don't you think so?"

They both looked so mournful, I found myself saying, "It's really okay. At least for us … well, me. I'm still stuffed from dinner."

"I am too," Jerome said.

I shot him a grateful look.

"Oh," Mildred said, perking up. "How WAS dinner?" She was back to leaning in toward us.

"Um, it was good," I said awkwardly, wondering if there was any way I could get out of the conversation. I turned toward Jerome to see if he could help, and I noticed a full glass of wine in front of me. When did that happen? He flashed me a smile as he nodded to the wine. "I thought you could use another."

I could have kissed him.

I seized the glass and took a long drink, not caring about it being way over my limit. Hey, it was Friday, after all. I deserved it. Plus, it was helping me focus less on Mildred and Aunt Tilde, who were still chattering at me. And to each other. And to the waitress. I hic-cupped and tried not to laugh as I carefully placed my wine down on the table that had suddenly started tipping.

And that was when I saw it. Over Jerome's shoulder.

I froze, my stomach sinking into my high-heeled sandals. It was Nick, standing in a small group of people, holding a beer. He appeared to be talking to one of them, a man dressed similarly to him in dress pants, a long-sleeve button-down shirt, and a tie that hung loosely around his neck. Trisha was also in the group, but she was talking to one of the women, who, like her, was dressed to the nines in a tiny red dress and very high heels.

How could this even be happening, I wondered. *I go out on a date and end up at the same place as Mildred, Aunt Tilde, Nick, and Trisha. I must be cursed.*

"Emily?" Jerome was staring at me, concern knitting his brows. "Are you okay?"

"Emily, what's going on?" Mildred screeched from the next table. I whirled toward her, suddenly panicked that Nick would hear, even over the din of the bar. In fact … *did* Nick flinch? Oh no. If he saw me …

"Nothing," I said to Mildred. "Everything is fine."

Mildred gave me a put-out expression. "Then why didn't you answer? I asked what you ate?"

"Um …" My mind went blank. I was still stuck on Nick just twenty feet away. Sure, he was talking to someone just then, but if he just turned his head slightly to the right …

"What did you say?" Mildred shrieked again, and I jumped, splashing red wine over my pink top. "Crap," I said, leaping to my feet. It was one of my favorites. I grabbed a napkin and started trying to mop it up.

"Don't rub it in," Mildred ordered. "You need to dab."

"We need some club soda. Right now," Aunt Tilde said, looking around wildly, as if it might just materialize in front of her.

"I'll just go to the bathroom," I said before realizing I had no idea where the bathroom was. Worse, what if I had to walk by Nick? Oh geez. Why did I ever agree to a drink? Never again.

"It's over there," Jerome said, pointing to the side of the bar. At least I could safely skirt around where Nick was standing. Finally, one thing that seemed to go my way.

"I'll be right back," I said as I headed toward the bathroom.

"Remember, don't rub!" Mildred shouted. "Dab."

"And find some club soda," Aunt Tilde yelled.

I flashed them the thumbs-up signal, hoping that would be enough to quiet them down, and hurried away as fast as I could on my teetering heels.

Chapter 6

I was able to get most of the wine out of my shirt, thank goodness. However, I also had a giant wet spot to show for it.

I studied myself in the mirror, trying to rearrange my clothes, but it didn't help. There was no hiding that half of my top was wet. Ugh.

But that wasn't the worst of it. My lipstick was gone, my mascara was smudged, and my feet were killing me thanks to the heels I had thought so sexy paired with a tight pair of jeans and my pink top. Now, I just looked like a drowned rat.

Well, maybe there was an upside. I could use it as an excuse to leave, before things got any worse (aka Nick seeing me). Actually, what would *really* be worse would be him seeing Aunt Tilde or Mildred.

Yikes. Just the thought of it made me want to lock myself in the bathroom all night, but that wasn't an option. With my luck, Trisha would come strolling in to fix her makeup.

That thought was enough to get me moving. I quickly dug my lipstick out of my purse and reapplied, then wet a paper towel to fix the smudges around my eyes. Finally, I ran my fingers through my hair, fluffing it up.

I surveyed the damage. Better, though not by much. Well, there also wasn't much to be done about it. I decided to leave before Trisha and her friend discovered me.

I opened the door and tottered back into the bar.

And nearly ran smack into Nick's broad chest.

I wobbled, and for a moment, it seemed I might topple over, which would just be the icing on the cake. Luckily, Nick reached out and grabbed my forearms, steadying me.

For a moment, we just stared at each other, before we both began talking at once.

"Excuse me," I said at the same time Nick said, "Emily, what are you doing here?"

He sounded flabbergasted by the idea of it—me, in a bar on a Friday night. Like it was such a shock I would have a social life. My back immediately stiffened. "Having a drink with a friend. Why, is there something wrong with that?"

He frowned. "No, why would you think that?"

"Because you sound surprised to see me." I winced at the sound of my voice. I sounded like a petulant child. For that matter, I felt like one, too. His hands were warm on my skin, too warm. I wanted him to let go of me. He shouldn't be touching me anyway, considering he was with Trisha.

But I didn't pull away.

He looked me up and down. "Why is your shirt wet?"

I winced. Of course he would notice. "I spilled wine on it."

He gave me a second look. "Are you drunk?"

That did make me yank my arms away. He let me go, and I almost tipped over again, but managed to catch myself. "You *are* drunk."

"I am not," I said hotly, although it probably would have sounded better if I hadn't slurred. "I just had a couple glasses of wine." Or three. Or four.

He folded his arms across his chest. "Uh huh. Just a couple."

He was teasing me. I could tell by the glint in his eyes, but for some reason, that made me even more mad. This night had already turned into enough of a train wreck; I didn't need him giving me grief for drinking. I glared at him. "Oh, give me a break. You're not my father."

He raised an eyebrow. "You're absolutely right. I'm not. And it's a good thing, with that outfit you're wearing. I'd have had to get my shotgun." He leered at me.

I slapped his arm, trying to ignore the warmth that was turning my insides into liquid. "Stop it. You're not funny."

"Oh, I have to disagree with you there. I think I'm very funny."

He was still standing too close—so close he was making me dizzy. Even his scent was intoxicating … that unique mixture of aftershave and shampoo with his maleness. I knew I had to get away, far away, but in order to do that, I had to get past him. "I … uh …"

"Emily! What's going on?"

Oh no. This can't be happening. I squeezed my eyes shut, hoping when I opened them, I'd be back in my little apartment above Aunt Tilde's garage.

"Wait, is that … *Mildred?*" If Nick sounded surprised before, now, he was downright astonished. Which meant I wasn't dreaming. I reluctantly opened my eyes only to see Mildred barreling toward us, Aunt Tilde struggling to keep up, and Nick watching them with a bewildered expression on his face.

"It's not what you think," I said weakly as Nick swung his head toward me, his jaw hanging open.

"You're here with Mildred? And Tilde?"

"No, I just told you, it's not what you think," I hissed as Mildred charged up to us.

"Emily! Why are you standing here talking to Nick when Jerome is waiting for you?"

Nick's expression didn't change, but I thought I saw his nostrils flair. "Oh, so you're here with Jerome."

"I told you it's not what you think," I muttered yet again.

"Emily!" Mildred was using her teacher's voice, and I found myself standing straighter. "Don't you think you should go back to your date?"

"Oh Mildred," Aunt Tilde said. "Joshua will be fine. He's a big boy. He can handle sitting there by himself for a minute."

Mildred turned her icy glare to Aunt Tilde. "It's *Jerome.*"

"Right. Jerome." Aunt Tilde fluttered her hands.

"Nick, what's taking you so … oh, Emily." Trisha appeared by Nick's side, her voice definitely cooler the moment she saw me. "I didn't realize you would be here tonight." She tucked a hand into the crook of Nick's arm.

I was suddenly exasperated. "Why is it such a surprise I'm at a bar on a Friday night?"

Trisha shrugged. "I don't know, you just don't seem like a … bar girl, is all."

I stared at her. "A 'bar girl'? What on earth is that?"

Trisha tilted her head as she examined her nails. "Well, you know. Someone who likes to party. Right, Nick?" She gazed up at him, an adoring expression on her face, but Nick was still staring at Mildred and Aunt Tilde, looking like he was witnessing his worst nightmare come to life.

"She's not a … a bar girl or a party girl," Mildred said, her voice a little huffy. "Emily is very responsible. Just because she's at a bar doesn't mean she isn't a responsible, respectful member of society."

While a part of me appreciated Mildred defending me, somehow, her defense made me sound even more like someone who would never go to a bar or have any sort of social life. "Why would being at a bar make you irresponsible?" I asked. "You're at a bar."

"My point exactly," Mildred sniffed.

Trisha's face had gone slack as she peered around Nick. "Wait. You're from The Redemption Detective Agency, aren't you? What are you doing here?" Her head swiveled around to me. "Is this who you're out with?" The disdain dripped from her voice as she looked me up and down. "And you're dressed like that?"

"What's wrong with us?" Mildred demanded, her hands on her hips. "We can't have a drink at a bar?"

"Besides, Emily is on a date," Aunt Tilde said. "We just happened to run into her."

Nick looked at the three of us. "You just happened to run into Emily having a date?" His voice was full of skepticism.

"Of course we did," Mildred said. "What, you think we're out here spying on Emily and Jerome on their first date?"

"Heaven forbid anyone think that," I said, trying not to roll my eyes.

"Did someone say my name?" Jerome had now joined our little group. He looked around at each of us, his eyes settling on Nick and his expression hardening. "Oh, hi Nate. I didn't realize you were here."

"It's Nick," Nick said, flashing Jerome a tight smile.

"Nick. Of course," Jerome said, with an equally forced grin. The two men stared at each other, like two predators sizing up their competition.

"We should probably go," I said to Jerome. The tension between them was so thick, it was becoming hard to breathe. On second thought, it wasn't just between Jerome and Nick, but the entire group. Everyone seemed to be scowling at someone else, and all the strain was starting to give me a headache.

"Sure, babe," Jerome said without looking at me.

I bristled. Babe? This was our first date! He hadn't even tried to kiss me yet! How could I possibly be "babe"? But before I could object, he slid his gaze toward me and flashed me a smile, and I felt my resistance thaw a bit.

"Good idea. Let's go back to our table," Mildred said.

"We can order another drink," Aunt Tilde said. "I'll buy."

Oh geez. That's all I needed. More wine and those two honing in on my date.

"Actually, I'm so sorry, but I should really get going," Jerome said, his voice sounding regretful. "I have to be up early for a meeting."

"A meeting? On a Saturday?" Aunt Tilde asked.

"It's a volunteer meeting," Jerome clarified. "I do some mentoring of at-risk boys in our community."

"And it's so good of you to do that," Mildred said, giving Aunt Tilde the side-eye. "I remember you talking about how much you enjoy working with those boys."

"Yes, there's nothing quite like watching them succeed despite their circumstances," Jerome said. In the corner of my eye, I could see Nick roll his eyes, and it suddenly occurred to me that Nick would have been considered one of those "at-risk boys." Based on his reaction, it didn't seem like Nick was a fan of this type of mentoring, although it was possible he just wasn't a fan of Jerome.

"Which is why I should probably call it a night and take you home," Jerome continued, offering me his arm. "Are you ready to go?"

"Absolutely," I said, keeping my eyes firmly on Jerome, so I wouldn't have to look at Mildred, Aunt Tilde, Trisha, or Nick, although I could feel Nick's eyes boring into the back of my neck as I walked out on Jerome's arm.

Chapter 7

"So, when is the stakeout?" Nora asked as she burst into the agency, Smoke sidling in beside her. He glanced first at Scout lying on his bed and then at Sherlock in her cat tower before slinking off into a corner to sulk.

Mildred shot me a pointed look over her coffee. "We're not sure. We're still waiting for the equipment."

Nora's face fell. "Oh. I was hoping we were going to start tonight. I baked cookies." She held up a container to show us.

Mildred grumbled something, but her expression had perked up some at the word "cookie." Which was good, because so far, the week was starting off with a thud.

It was Monday morning, and Mildred had showed up bright and early (which, in Mildred's world, meant sometime before noon), ostensibly because she wanted to get comfortable with all the stakeout equipment that she somehow believed had magically arrived over the weekend. Though it was possible she believed a magic camera fairy had visited us, I think what she really wanted was to pepper me with questions about my date.

When I informed her she had a choice—I could either answer her questions or get the stakeout equipment ordered—she went off in a huff to make a pot of coffee to presumably drown her frustrations in.

"Well thank you, Nora. That was sweet of you," Aunt Tilde said, helping herself to a cookie. "Emily, can I bring you one?"

I shot her the evil eye before declining, as politely as I could muster, which I didn't think was all that polite. I was still upset with her about what happened Friday night. When I confronted her over the weekend about how she could have possibly thought crashing my date was a good idea, she tried to dismiss it. "We just wanted a drink at The Tipsy Cow," she insisted.

"At eleven o'clock at night?" I asked in disbelief. "You're never out that late."

"Well, not usually," Aunt Tilde said. "But it was a Friday night, and we wanted to celebrate."

"Celebrate what?" If she said the fact I was on a date …

"Our new client, of course," Aunt Tilde said. "It's exciting to have a real, paying client. Not to mention we get to go on a real-life stakeout."

"You could have celebrated earlier," I said.

"Oh, what's the fun in that?" Aunt Tilde asked, waving her hands.

I narrowed my eyes and put my hands on my hips. "And of course, the fact you were at The Tipsy Cow had nothing to do with Jerome and I being there."

"How would we even know you were there?" she countered.

"Maybe because Jerome told Mildred we might go there after dinner," I said.

Aunt Tilde waved her hands again. "If you know that, then what's the big deal? If Jerome is going to tell Mildred what you two are doing, why should it be such a surprised if she shows up?"

I closed my eyes and slowly counted to ten.

"Besides, you should be thanking me," she continued.

I pried one eye open to look at her. "*Thanking* you?"

"Absolutely," Aunt Tilde said, nodding her head. "If it were up to Mildred, she would have showed up at Mario's for dinner, but I told her it would be better to wait until you were at The Tipsy Cow. A bar is far less intrusive, don't you think?"

I had no answer to that. But that didn't mean I wasn't still irked at both of them.

"How was your date?" Aunt Tilde asked.

"Fine."

She raised an eyebrow. "Only fine?"

I didn't answer, choosing instead to throw her a pointed look before turning on my heel and striding away. If she thought I was going to give her *any* details after the stunt she and Mildred had pulled, she was sorely mistaken.

The truth was, the date was fine. More than fine, actually. At least until everyone and their brother showed up at The Tipsy Cow. I had really enjoyed spending time with Jerome. I even started to think there might be something there. Despite all that had happened at the bar, he had been a perfect gentleman to the end—walking me to my door and giving me a chaste kiss on the cheek.

But there was no talk of a second date. He had apologized, profusely, for telling Mildred his plan, and promised never to do it again (which was a good sign, right? Surely, there would be no reason to promise to never tell Mildred again if he had no intention of seeing me a second time), but nothing else.

I tried to not let it bother me. After all, could I blame him if he didn't want anything to do with me? Obviously, I came with baggage, and even if Mildred and Aunt Tilde didn't crash any more dates, he was still going to come in contact with them from time to time. I needed to let him decide if he wanted to deal with all of that or not.

But that didn't mean I had to share the details of my date with either Mildred or Aunt Tilde. As far as I was concerned, they could just suffer. Just like I was.

"Okay, so if we can't go on the stakeout today, can we do it tomorrow?" Nora asked.

"That's up to Emily," Aunt Tilde said. "Emily, what do you say? Can we do the stakeout tomorrow?"

You've got to be kidding me. I lifted my head to see all three women staring at me with various eager expressions. With a sigh, I put my pen down and straightened up. Now was as good as time as any to give them an update, and besides, I had a feeling that until I did, I wasn't going to get anything done.

"So, I'm almost done with the initial research," I said. "It's taking me a little longer than normal because I don't have a lot of experience with cameras or microphones, so I wanted to make sure I was being thorough."

"Of course," Aunt Tilde said. "We want you to be thorough."

"But not too thorough," Mildred said.

"Why wouldn't we want her to be too thorough?" Nora asked. "Isn't being thorough a good thing?"

"Yes, unless it takes too long," Mildred said. "We did make promises to our client."

Inwardly, I winced. They had indeed made promises I wish they hadn't, and I tried to walk back. I wasn't sure how successful I was. "Mildred is right. It is a balance between researching enough so you feel confident about your purchase and not taking so long that it wastes a bunch of time. Which is why I should be finishing up in another hour or so …"

"And then you'll order everything?" Mildred interrupted, her eyes lighting up. She turned to Nora. "So we should be able to do the stakeout tomorrow after all!"

Nora clapped her hands. "Yay!"

"Actually, that's not quite right," I said.

Mildred jerked her head back to me. "What do you mean? You said you're almost done researching."

"Yes …"

"And then, the next step would be ordering the equipment."

"Not exactly," I said as all three of their faces fell. I was starting to feel like a parent telling their children that no, they can't start with dessert; they need to eat their dinner first. "I was going to prepare a presentation on my top choices for each piece of equipment, so you can decide which ones you want."

"Oh, a presentation," Aunt Tilde said, her expression brightening. The three of them looked at each other, and I could see the mental struggle between watching a presentation and getting the equipment faster.

"If it helps," I said, "it's still possible we could have it by tomorrow. Depending on what you decide, there might be some stores in Riverview that have what we want in stock. And if that's the case, we could just drive there tomorrow and pick it up."

"Sold," Aunt Tilde said. "Let's do it."

"Agreed," Mildred said. "Stakeout tomorrow."

"I'll bake more cookies," Nora said.

"Yes, but we don't know …" I started to say, but then I gave up. Maybe purchasing everything locally and moving on was the best thing we could do. For all I knew, we might never do another stakeout, in which case, it really didn't matter what we bought.

"So, when are you going to have the presentation ready?" Aunt Tilde asked.

"In a few hours." I glanced at the clock. "I'm guessing after lunch, like maybe two or three o'clock."

"Perfect. Meeting at two," Aunt Tilde said, looking at Nora and Mildred, who nodded.

Apparently, I was going to be done at two, which meant I needed to make sure they stayed out of my hair. "But in the meantime," I said. "Have you reviewed Jan's file?"

"What's there to review?" Mildred asked. "We just need that cheating jerk's photo and place of employment, so we can catch him in the act."

"Alleged cheater," I said. "We don't know if he's cheating on Jan or not."

Mildred blinked at me. "Of course we know. Jan told us he is."

"Jan told us she thinks he's cheating on her," I said. "There's a difference."

Mildred looked at me in confusion. "So you don't think he's a cheating sleazeball?"

"He might not be a sleazeball," Nora said. "He could just be a cheater."

"If he's cheating on her, he's a sleazeball," Mildred said.

I spread my arms out. "I think we should be a little objective. We were hired to investigate, not make assumptions."

"Emily is right," Aunt Tilde said. "We owe it to our client to approach our cases objectively."

"Correct. I don't think we should assume he's cheating on Jan without catching him in the act," I said. "I think we should keep an open mind about every part of this case."

Based on the bewildered look all three women were giving me, my message was clearly not landing. "What do we know about Jan?"

"Jan?" Mildred's perplexed expression deepened. "What do you mean? She's our client."

"I know that, but don't you think her manner was a little … off?"

"Well, of course it was," Mildred said. "Her husband is a cheating sleazeball."

"Again, we don't actually know he's a … he's cheating, until we investigate," I said.

"Which is what we're going to do," Mildred said. "Investigate."

I was definitely not getting my point across.

"Emily, what exactly are you trying to say?" Aunt Tilde asked me, her brows bunching on her forehead.

I took a deep breath, deciding maybe I should just spit it out. "I'm just not sure we should have taken this case."

Nora looked at me in horror. "But then we couldn't do a stake-out."

"I know," I said. "And that would be unfortunate."

"But why shouldn't we have?" Aunt Tilde asked.

"Because …" I paused as I tried to figure out a way to way to explain that I had a bad feeling about her without saying, "I have a bad feeling about her."

"Because …" Aunt Tilde prompted.

"Well, it's just …" I stuttered, feeling like I was fumbling around in the dark. "It's like I said before, there is something off with her."

"Again, she thinks her husband is cheating on her," Mildred said. "Not to mention she's just taken a big step toward proving it by hiring us. Wouldn't you seem off, too, if you just did that?"

I had to admit, Mildred had a point.

"But it's more than that," I said, "What about how interested she was in the Duckworths?"

Mildred shrugged. "Everyone's interested in the Duckworths. They're practically celebrities." She sniffed. "Not that they deserve it. Especially after the way they treated you."

"I completely agree," Aunt Tilde said as Nora bobbed her head. Even Scout raised his head from his dog bed and looked over at me, his tail thumping against the floor.

A faint warmth filled my chest. For so much of my life, I had been alone, fighting my own battles, rarely having anyone on my side. Not my former fiancé, and certainly not my mother. Only Aunt Tilde had ever stood by me, no matter what happened.

And now, not only did I have Aunt Tilde, but apparently, I also had Mildred, Nora, and even Scout in my corner.

"I appreciate that," I said, clearing my throat as I fiddled with the papers on my desk. "And while I agree with you, about the Duckworths I mean, I still found Jan's reaction a little ... excessive. Didn't you?"

"Maybe she was just trying to make conversation," Nora said. "It's like that book about making friends. She was showing interest in topics that interest you."

Considering I had been trying everything possible to get Jan to change the subject (other than being completely rude, that is), I didn't see how Nora could possibly think she was merely being conversational with me. "But didn't you find something off with the way she was acting?" I asked.

All three of them stared at me like I had grown a third head. "I don't understand," Nora finally said. "How did you want her to act?"

"She thinks her husband is cheating on her," Aunt Tilde added. "People do strange things when they're in the middle of an emotional crisis."

That gave me pause. Was I being too harsh on Jan? How is one supposed to act when they think their spouse is getting ready to leave them? Maybe I should give Jan a break, even though every time I thought about the almost hungry expression on her face when she pushed me for gossip on the Duckworths gave me a chill.

"Maybe you're right," I said. "To me, it just felt like she was getting ready to ask me to set her up with one of the Duckworths. And even if she is planning on getting divorced, she's not divorced now, so it seems a little ... premature."

"A little planning is never a bad idea," Mildred said. "Especially at her age. She's not getting any younger, so if she thinks she can land a Duckworth, she's going to have to move quickly. Not that she should want one, but to each his own, I always say."

"Oh, we can't let her do that," Nora said. "That would be horrible. We need to tell her that the Duckworths aren't trustworthy."

"Hold on," I said, holding a hand up. "I'm not comfortable with that."

Nora wrung her hands together. "I'm not saying we tell her your story. Maybe we just tell her we know someone who all of this happened to. Someone she doesn't know."

"I don't think that's a great idea," I said.

"Well, we need to do something," Nora said.

The conversation was not going the way I had hoped, but I wasn't sure how to get it back on track. "So first of all, we don't even know if Jan is going to get divorced," I said. "It's possible her husband isn't cheating on her after all."

"Unlikely," Mildred said.

"But still possible," I said.

"Emily is right," Aunt Tilde said. "We should first find out if her husband is even doing it. If he is, then we can decide how to warn her off the Duckworths, too. Deal?"

"Deal," Mildred and Nora both agreed. All three of them looked expectantly at me.

"Deal," I said faintly. How had I managed to screw up this conversation so badly? I'd started it hoping to talk them out of taking Jan as a client, but it seemed all I had managed to do was make them even more committed to helping her.

Chapter 8

"Emily, have you eaten yet?" Aunt Tilde peered at me from over her orange-rimmed glasses.

I glanced at the clock. It was nearly twelve-thirty. "No, but I'm fine." As soon as I said it, my stomach growled, and I realized I wasn't. Breakfast had consisted of a couple of pieces of toast, hastily scarfed down before hurrying into work, and the gallons of coffee I had been drinking didn't exactly count.

"You should eat," Aunt Tilde said.

"Yes, you should," Mildred echoed, before pursing her lips. "You're already too thin."

Inwardly, I rolled my eyes. I was absolutely not too thin, although I appreciated the sentiment. "I need about fifteen minutes before I finish this."

Mildred's eyes lit up. "Oh. Yes, you should definitely finish your presentation first."

Aunt Tilde shot her a look.

"What?" Mildred asked, her face innocent. "I'm simply encouraging her to get her work done before she takes a break."

"She needs to eat," Aunt Tilde insisted before turning back to me. "You need to eat. You work too hard."

"And I will," I said. "In about fifteen minutes."

"We should leave her alone," Mildred said, rising from her chair. "Tilde, we haven't had lunch either. Maybe we should eat now, and by the time we get back, Emily will be ready for her lunch break."

"Yes, that's an excellent idea," I said. While the two of them had, more or less, left me alone, their constant chatting was a distraction. I was getting better at tuning them out, but having them out of the agency would be better yet.

"Perfect," Mildred said, picking up her purse. "We'll be back in a jiffy. Tilde?"

Aunt Tilde was still sitting at her desk, a less-than-pleased expression on her face. "I don't know about this," she fretted. "Emily, you're the one who needs a break. You've been working hard all morning."

"And the sooner we get out of her hair, the faster she'll finish," Mildred said.

"Mildred is right," I said, even though I could hardly believe Mildred and I were on the same side. "You two go have lunch, and I'll take a lunch break when you get back."

Aunt Tilde still didn't look convinced, but she reluctantly stood up. "I feel like we're abusing you," she said.

"Trust me, you're not."

"Can we at least bring you a sandwich or something?" Aunt Tilde asked.

"Sure, that would be great." The longer they stood there arguing about lunch, the hungrier I was starting to feel, and I truly did want to get the presentation finished.

I had barely gotten my focus back when I heard the little bell ring above the door. With a sigh, I raised my head, sure it was either Aunt Tilde or Mildred with a question that could be as mundane as what kind of sandwich I wanted to something as outlandish as whether it was a misdemeanor or felony to break into someone's home.

But it wasn't Aunt Tilde or Mildred. It was Trisha.

"Trisha," I said after managing to close my mouth that had fallen open. I straightened, running a hand through my hair, wishing I had done something other than throw it back in a messy ponytail that morning. "Um, Nick isn't here."

Trisha gave me a faint smile that looked forced. "I'm not here to see him."

"Oh? Well …" I looked around the agency, even though I already knew the only ones there were Sherlock, Scout, and myself. "Aunt Tilde and Mildred aren't here either …"

"I'm here to see you," she said, looking directly at me.

There was something in her eyes, something I couldn't identify, that was making me nervous. I was starting to wish I hadn't chased Mildred and Aunt Tilde out. Was she going to accuse me of something? Maybe something to do with Nick? But that was silly. Nick and I were just friends ... or something. Co-workers maybe? Although we didn't exactly work together. What if I referred to him as an associate? Trisha couldn't object to that, could she? "Oh. Um ... how can I help you?"

She didn't immediately answer. Instead, she started digging around in her purse. She was dressed in a smart navy suit consisting of a pencil skirt and a fitted jacket. Her black hair was pulled back in a bun, and her makeup was more subtle than what I normally saw her wear, at least when she was going out with Nick. "It's about Friday night," she said as she continued rooting around in her bag.

My mouth went dry. Why did she want to talk to me about Friday night? Was she about to warn me away from Nick? Why would she do that? Just because she saw us talking? But that was absurd. Didn't she realize I was on a date? And besides, even if I wasn't, Nick and I were just ... whatever. Associates or something.

"Um, about that ..." I started to say, even though I hadn't a clue what the rest of the sentence would be. But it didn't matter, because Trisha suddenly turned toward me, flinging her hand out.

"Is this yours?" she asked abruptly.

I stared at her, blinking. The question was so far from what I thought she was going to say, it took me a minute to even comprehend what she was asking. "What?"

"This. Is it yours?" She took a step toward me, shaking her fist. Now that she was closer, I noticed the bags under her eyes and the paleness of her skin, despite the thick foundation she had used in an attempt to conceal them. She waved her fist again, and I tore my gaze away to see what she was holding. It looked like a piece of jewelry.

"What is it?" Whatever it was, it sparkled under the light, all gold and diamonds.

She looked at me like I was an idiot. "It's an earring."

I blinked and focused again. "Oh, yeah, I see it now. It's kind of ..." I swallowed hard. A part of me was thinking garish, but considering the circumstances, I didn't think that was very polite. "It kind of dangles."

She blew the air out of her mouth like she was trying to rein in her temper. "Is it yours or not?"

I shook my head, even as I wondered how she could possibly think I would wear something like that. My current earrings were respectful diamond studs. Maybe, for a special occasion, I would add some small gold or silver hoops, but that was really it.

"Oh. Okay, just checking." She stuffed the earring back into her purse, and that seemed to be the end of the conversation.

"That's … that's why you're here?"

She was still rummaging in her purse and didn't look at me. "Yep."

This couldn't be real. I must be misunderstanding … something. "You came all this way to ask me about that earring?"

"It wasn't that out of my way," Trisha said, her voice matter of fact. Although she still wasn't looking at me. "Besides, I'm on my lunch break."

It still seemed an extraordinary thing for her to do, especially given the fact I would barely call us acquaintances, much less friends. "But why would you think it was mine?"

"I found it at The Tipsy Cow after you left. I thought maybe you lost it."

"Oh." That seemed like such a thoughtful gesture, which also seemed peculiar for Trisha. "Well, um … it's not. But thank you for checking?" Should I even be thanking her? This was just getting more and more bizarre. Where were Mildred and Aunt Tilde with my sandwich … or whatever it was they were going to end up bringing me? With them, you could never be too sure what you would get. For all I knew, I might end up with a nice set of lock picks rather than lunch.

"No problem." She sounded like she was the one doing me the favor, and I had to stop myself from thanking her for stopping by. "I'll see you around."

"Sure. See you," I said, watching her walk toward the door.

Her hand was on the handle when she suddenly turned back to me. "Oh, I almost forgot." She looked flustered. "I wanted to tell you. I was wrong about my aunt."

It took me a moment for my brain to catch up to the new conversation twist. "Your aunt? You mean … her missing dog?"

"Yeah, that." She swallowed, her eyes still not meeting mine. "I was wrong. She didn't have a dog."

For a moment, I could only stare at her. "I'm sorry, you're telling me you were … wrong about your aunt having a dog?"

She nodded. A dull, unflattering shade of red had risen up her neck. "Yeah. I was confused and thinking of my other aunt."

Had I fallen into an episode of *The Twilight Zone*? How could this conversation have gotten even stranger? "Wait a minute. You're saying you have another aunt who has a dog that went missing? For a year?"

The redness crept to her chin. "No, that's not what I meant. I thought … well, it doesn't matter. I misunderstood what Aunt Gin told me, is all. So, anyway, I'm sorry for wasting your time."

"But I still don't …"

"Errr, look at the time. Sorry, I gotta go," Trisha's voice sang out as she flung open the front door and practically ran out, nearly tripping on her high heels and leaving me sitting in total disbelief as I wondered what exactly had happened.

Chapter 9

I was still sitting in the same place, staring at the same door, mouth hanging open while trying to make sense of what happened when Mildred and Aunt Tilde walked back in. "Emily, we have your sandwich," Aunt Tilde sang out.

"It's tuna," Mildred said, wrinkling her nose. She wasn't a fan. She would often complain about the smell. "You like roast beef better, though. Don't you?"

"She likes tuna," Aunt Tilde insisted, plopping the white bag in front of me.

"Tuna is fine," I said absently, my mind still on what had happened with Trisha. "Or roast beef. I like both."

Mildred folded her arms across her chest and glared at Aunt Tilde. "I told you roast beef would have been better."

Aunt Tilde waved her hands at her. "But tuna was the special, so of course it's better." She turned to me. "Did you get everything done?"

Mildred's eyes lit up. "Yes, the presentation. Can we see it?"

"Yeah, it's done. Basically," I said, reaching for the bag, my stomach growling again. I still wasn't really listening to either of them, but my stomach was insisting that I put some food in it.

"Basically?" Mildred asked, her eyebrows going up.

"Can we see it?" Aunt Tilde asked at the same time.

"Yeah, sure," I said, unwrapping the sandwich and taking a huge bite. "Trisha was here," I said around a mouthful of food.

"Trisha?" Aunt Tilde asked, frowning. "Why would Trisha be here? Is Nick here?"

Mildred flapped her hands impatiently. "Oh, never mind her. We can talk about her later. We need to order that equipment."

"Right," I said, taking another bite of my sandwich before putting it down to organize my notes. I was going to make copies for everyone, but I had a feeling Mildred might hurt herself if she had to wait much longer. "No, Nick isn't here. She wanted to talk to me."

That got Mildred's attention. "You? Why did she want to talk to you?" Her eyes narrowed suspiciously. "She knows you're dating Jerome, right?"

"I guess," I said, wondering myself if I was dating Jerome, since he hadn't called me back. "She did see us together Friday night."

Mildred sniffed. "That doesn't mean she doesn't know he's off limits. I hope you made that clear to her."

I stared at her as what she was saying finally sunk in. "Wait a minute. You think that Trisha is interested in Jerome?" I wasn't sure if I wanted to laugh or cry at the ridiculousness of it.

Mildred looked at me in surprise. "Of course she is. Why wouldn't she want to trade up from Nick?" Her voice dripped with disdain.

"He's not so bad," I said. For a defense, it wasn't great, but I had to say something. I knew Mildred didn't like Nick—she was sure he was a womanizer who would break my heart if I gave him a half the chance. And while it was possible she was right, I also thought she was being a little too hard on him. Especially when I thought of all the good things he had been doing, not just for Aunt Tilde and The Redemption Detective Agency, but also for … me.

"Be glad you don't know him the way I do," Mildred said ominously.

"Oh, for heaven's sake," Aunt Tilde said. "Give the boy a break. It's not his fault he's too good looking by half. He can't help it when women throw themselves at him."

True enough, I thought.

"Besides," Aunt Tilde continued. "That still doesn't explain why Trisha was here."

"She was trying to steal Emily's boyfriend," Mildred said. "Right, Emily?"

"What? No, that's not why she was here." Sometimes, I truly did want to strangle Mildred. "It had nothing to do with men or dating."

"Then what was she doing here?" Aunt Tilde asked again.

"It was about her aunt's dog," I said. "Or, I should say, her lack of a dog."

"You mean her cousin's dog," Mildred said.

I gritted my teeth and plowed on. "Trisha told me she'd been confused. Her aunt doesn't have a dog after all."

"What have I been telling you?" Mildred asked, her voice full of satisfaction. "You should have listened to me."

Aunt Tilde's brow furrowed. "So it was Trisha's cousin who owned the dog? I was sure she told us it was her aunt."

Breathe, I whispered to myself. "Yes, that's what she said. She told us her Aunt Gin owned a dog who disappeared a year ago, but when I went to her aunt's house, she told me she never owned a dog before. Only Rocky, which is the dog she has now. And now, Trisha is saying that she was confused, and no, her aunt Gin never did own a dog before Rocky."

"So, there's no problem, then," Aunt Tilde said. "No dog, no case?"

"Well, technically," I said, wondering why this was so difficult. "But don't you think it's weird that a niece thinks her aunt owns a dog when she doesn't?"

"Maybe she's estranged from her aunt," Mildred said.

"But then why did she think the dog disappeared in the first place?" I asked.

"Because she was confused. Like she said," Mildred said.

"She was confused whether one of her family members owned a dog or not?" I asked.

Mildred pressed her lips together and lowered her voice to a stage whisper, even though there was no one else in the office. "I don't know if you noticed, but Trisha isn't very bright."

Every now and then, Mildred says exactly the right thing.

"It's possible she did get something mixed up and is remembering it wrong," Aunt Tilde said. "It happens. I had a friend once who was sure her brother-in-law had died, and then one day he showed up on her doorstep. He wanted to borrow her lawnmower. Almost gave her a heart attack."

"I thought it was her snowblower," Mildred said.

"I'm sure it was her lawnmower," Aunt Tilde said. "I remember Priscilla saying how he kept talking about how overgrown his lawn was because his mower had broken, and he couldn't get it fixed. She kept thinking it was some ghostly humor because he was supposed to be pushing up daisies."

"No, it couldn't be summer," Mildred said. "I remember her talking about how frozen he looked … like he was some mythical ice zombie that had come to eat her brains."

"Wait, what?" I asked, wondering if I had heard Mildred right. She typically wasn't so … colorful.

"An ice zombie," Mildred said, her voice dry and objective, like she was explaining the latitude and longitude of Brazil. "Who had come to eat …"

"Oh, Priscilla wouldn't have said that," Aunt Tilde scoffed. "I doubt she even knew what a zombie is, much less an ice zombie. Is there even such a thing?"

"That's exactly what I told her," Mildred said. "There was no such thing as an ice zombie. Zombies are strictly tropical. Otherwise, they would be too frozen to move."

"How does one think their brother-in-law died when he's not dead?" I asked, changing the subject. The last thing I wanted to listen to was an in-depth discussion of various types of zombies.

"Priscilla was always a little flighty," Mildred said, before giving me a meaningful look.

"Well, yes, but in this case, it wasn't entirely her fault," Aunt Tilde said. "She didn't have a great relationship with her sister. They barely spoke, and when they did, they usually ended up arguing about something that happened thirty years ago. And whoever told Priscilla clearly got the details wrong."

"Or Priscilla got the details wrong," Mildred muttered. Aunt Tilde flashed her a look.

"So no one had died, then?" I asked.

"Oh, no," Aunt Tilde said. "Someone died, but it wasn't Priscilla's brother-in-law. It was Priscilla's sister's brother-in-law." She cocked her head. "I think that's who it was. Regardless, it was all very confusing, but it eventually got sorted out."

"That's good, I guess," I said faintly.

"But my point being," Aunt Tilde said, her voice perking up, "if you can have a misunderstanding around a dead brother-in-law, then obviously, a missing dog isn't a stretch."

"True," I said, even though it still didn't feel right to me. I kept picturing the expression on Gin's face—how she blanched when I brought up a dog from the past. It was almost like she was horrified someone was asking her about it. If it was a simple mix-up, would that have been her reaction? "But if it was just a misunderstanding on Trisha's part, wouldn't Gin act more … puzzled, or confused?"

"You mean she wasn't confused?" Aunt Tilde asked. "Didn't you say she didn't know what you were talking about?"

"Well, yes, but …" I said.

"Sounds like confusion to me," Mildred said.

"Yes, but it was more than confusion …" I said before trailing off. Even to my own ears, I was starting to sound ridiculous. Aunt Tilde and Mildred were right. This probably was just one giant misunderstanding.

Aunt Tilde was studying me, her eyes sharp. "What, Emily?"

I gave myself a quick shake. "Nothing."

"What were you going to say?" Aunt Tilde pressed.

I chewed on my bottom lip. "I guess that she seemed more … frightened than confused."

"Maybe she was frightened that Trisha could make such a mistake," Mildred said. "Or she was frightened because memory problems run in their family, and she was worried Trisha was having issues."

I hadn't thought about that. "I guess that could explain it."

Aunt Tilde patted my hand. "You're a good girl, Emily. You have good instincts. I think Mildred is correct—there's probably something else going on that your question triggered, but it had nothing to do with a missing dog."

"You're probably right," I said, straightening up and telling myself to stop thinking about it. Whatever was going on, it was none of my business. "Why don't one of you grab Nora, and let's make some decisions on stake-out equipment."

Chapter 10

I pushed open the door to The Brew House, the ice-cold air conditioning immediately cooling my sweaty cheeks. I breathed in the rich scents of coffee in all its various forms and began to feel the tight knot lodged between my shoulder blades slowly unwind.

When I had left the agency, Mildred, Aunt Tilde, and Nora were still discussing equipment options, although I wasn't sure if "discussion" was precisely the right word. I had pared each recommendation down to either two or three options and ranked each one, as well, so they knew which one I thought was best. Aunt Tilde loved it all and wanted to just move forward with my top recommendations. Mildred, however, wanted to look into some of the other products and do her own research, in case I had "missed" something. And Nora didn't really care what we bought; she was more interested in what she should bring to the upcoming stakeout.

After listening to them for a bit, I decided a walk to The Brew House for a latte was in order. I'd leave them to hash everything out while I enjoyed a little exercise and a much-needed break. I deserved it, as I had been working on that project for hours.

My intention was to think about nothing other than how delightful it was to be outside on a beautiful summer day. Instead, I found myself obsessing over Trisha, Gin, and a dog that may or may not exist and may or may not have gone missing throughout the entire walk.

No matter how much I told myself that Aunt Tilde and Mildred were likely right about Trisha, and it was just some sort of weird misunderstanding or general forgetfulness, I still felt that niggling sensation—something wasn't adding up.

I kept reminding myself it was truly far more likely that Trisha had mixed up which family member owned a dog (wouldn't it be something if Mildred was right, and it ended up being some unnamed cousin?) or, also according to Mildred, had even dreamed the whole thing up. Mildred mentioned, quite casually during a kerfuffle involving Scout and Smoke, (which required a badly needed correction), that Trisha probably dreamed the whole missing dog situation up. Apparently, as a child, she used to have dreams so vivid she was sure they were real.

"Heavens, I remember one time, Trisha came to school convinced that Russians were hiding under her bed," Mildred said.

I blinked at her. "Russians? Why would she think there were Russians under her bed? Wouldn't just a regular ol' monster do?"

"Oh, you have to remember, this was years ago. During the Cold War. Everyone thought there were Russians hiding under the bed," Mildred said, waving her hand. "You probably don't remember."

I was about to tell her that I was basically the same age as Trisha, and yes, I did remember the Cold War, but I certainly didn't remember anyone worrying about Russians under beds. However, since the Scout/Smoke situation had been put to rest, I went back to the presentation instead.

But now, thinking about it, I wondered how possible it could really be that Trisha dreamed the whole thing. It seemed ridiculous to entertain it happening as an adult, but I also didn't know her at all. Regardless, that still seemed a more likely explanation than what I kept coming back to every time I pictured Gin's horrified face in the doorway … or remembered the feeling I got when Gin told me she never had a dog before Rocky.

The feeling that she was lying.

But that made no sense. Why would she possibly lie to me about owning a dog? The whole thing was absurd.

Was she worried I would judge her for losing her dog? I mean, stuff happens. People make mistakes, and sometimes, those mistakes lead to awful consequences. It's sad, but nothing she should be ashamed of. It also seemed absurd that Gin wouldn't know that, but why else would she lie?

My mind kept trying to find another explanation as I ordered my latte and headed over to the counter to add sugar—real sugar, not that artificial crap. I made a face at the little pink and blue envelopes as I tore open a sugar packet and added its contents to my coffee. I deserved a treat, even if did go straight to my hips. Plus, I *had* walked to the shop, so that should count for something …

"Emily?"

I whirled around, still holding the open sugar envelope in one hand and leaving a trail of rogue sugar crystals on the ground. Nick was standing by the counter, paying for his coffee.

"Oh, hi," I said, feeling flustered and wishing I had taken a moment to freshen up my lipstick and maybe comb out my hair before heading over. I busied myself trying to finish putting sugar in my coffee, but the envelope was empty. I quickly grabbed another and started to tear it open.

"I didn't think they let you out of the agency, at least for something as mundane as coffee," Nick said, his voice close to my ear. I jumped, and my fingers slipped. The packet exploded in my hands, sending sugar flying everywhere.

"Oh my gosh, I'm so sorry," I babbled, catching the eye of one of the workers behind the counter. She smiled and waved at me as if to indicate it was no big deal.

"A little coffee with your sugar?" Nick asked, raising an eyebrow as I grabbed yet another packet.

I frowned at him. "You scared me."

"How could I scare you?" Nick asked in disbelief. "You saw me coming over to you."

I decided to ignore that and focused on doctoring my coffee. "What are you doing here anyway? This place isn't that close to your office."

Nick shrugged. "It's not that far either. Not like anything in Redemption is that far. But it's worth the trip for the best coffee in town." He smiled at me, and I felt my stomach flip. He was close enough that I could smell his distinctive scent, mixed with the woodsiness of his soap and the musk of his aftershave. I grabbed another packet of sugar, trying to distract myself.

"How did your date go?" Nick asked, his mouth puckering on the word "date" like he was tasting a lemon versus coffee.

"It was fine. What about yours? Did you have a nice time with Trisha?" Ugh. I had the same sour note in my voice when I said her name.

His lips twitched up into a half-smile. "It was fine," he said, mimicking my words. "So, when are you planning to see Jeremiah again?"

"It's Jerome, and none of your business." I squashed down the instant doubt that surfaced, as I hadn't heard from him yet. *Just because he still hasn't called doesn't mean he isn't interested*, I told myself. *It's only been a few days.*

His lips quirked up again in as he sipped his coffee. "How much sugar are you going to add?"

I dropped my gaze to the cup and the opened sugar packet in my hand. I had completely lost count as to how much I'd added, but it was too late now. I dumped it in and started stirring. "How long have you known Trisha?" The words were out of my mouth before I even realized what I was doing, but Mildred's explanations, and Trisha's strange behavior, kept swirling through my head. If anyone could give me some insight into Trisha, it would be Nick. Assuming he would be willing to.

Nick's eyes narrowed as he took another sip of coffee. I tasted mine as well. Ugh. Way too sweet. I tried not to make a face as I lowered it.

"Long enough," he said finally. "Why do you want to know?"

I shrugged. "Just curious. She stopped by today, and I was …"

Nick held up a hand. "Hold on. Trisha stopped by? As in stopped by the agency?"

I nodded as I did my best to keep my expression neutral. Nick suddenly seemed disconcerted, and I wondered why. "Yes. What else would I mean?"

He ran a hand roughly through his hair. "Was she looking for me?"

I stared at him, bemused. "No, she wanted to talk to me."

He looked so alarmed, it was all I could do to keep from bursting out laughing. "She wanted to talk to you? Why?"

"What, you think it's so surprising that someone would want to talk to me?" I asked, widening my eyes.

He ran his hand through his hair again. "Well, no. Of course not." His voice was cautious. "Is that why she stopped by?"

For a moment, I wavered between continuing to tease him versus getting the answers I was dying for. Almost reluctantly, I said, "No, she had found an earring at The Tipsy Cow and wanted to know if it was mine."

"Oh." He looked so relieved, I had to wonder why. Why would he care so much if Trisha stopped by to talk to me? Did that mean he was hiding something, and if he was, what? "Had you lost an earring?"

"No, but she also made a point of telling me that she was wrong about her aunt's dog going missing." I watched Nick's face carefully, as it suddenly occurred to me that maybe Nick knew more about Gin and her dog than he had let on, but he seemed only mildly interested.

"So the dog wasn't missing then?"

I frowned. That wasn't the response I was expecting. "No, she told me Gin never had a dog."

He gave me a puzzled look. "What are you talking about? I thought I heard you say she does."

"Yes, she has one now. But it's not the same one she had a year ago."

He still looked confused. "So the dog is still missing then?"

"No. I mean yes. I mean …" Ugh. Why did this have to be so complicated? "I mean apparently, there was no dog."

He stared at me, bewildered. "You just said she had a dog."

I glanced up at the ceiling and counted to ten. "Okay, let me start from the beginning. Trisha told us her aunt Gin had a dog that went missing a year ago."

"Right," Nick said, nodding.

"And when I went to talk to Gin, she told me she didn't have a dog a year ago, which would mean nothing had gone missing."

His brows knit together. "But that makes no sense. Trisha told me …" His face screwed up like he was thinking deeply. I held my breath, waiting for him to finish the sentence. Was I finally going to hear some proof that Gin was lying? But alas, that was not to be the case. Rather than continuing, Nick just gave himself a quick shake. "Okay, so why did Trisha stop by today? Other than to ask you if you lost an earring."

"She wanted to tell me that she had been wrong about Gin."

"Wrong how? That the dog hadn't gone missing after all?"

"That Gin never had a dog. At least," I amended, "before Rocky, which is the dog she has now."

Nick stared at me in silence. I could almost see the wheels turning. "Let me get this straight," he finally said. "Trisha first told you that her aunt Gin had a dog go missing a year ago, and now, she's saying she was wrong, and her aunt never had a dog."

"Yes." Finally, someone who seemed to be as baffled about it as I was. Maybe I wasn't crazy after all. I was so relieved, I wanted to kiss him, and I immediately felt my face flush at the thought of it. No, I wasn't going there. Hurriedly, I took another swallow of my latte and almost choked on the sweetness.

Luckily, Nick didn't seem to notice, as he still seemed stuck on the dog discrepancy. "Did Trisha tell you why she was changing her story?"

"Not really. Just that she got it wrong."

Nick frowned. "That's weird. I wonder why Gin wanted her to lie."

Was he saying what I thought he was? I could barely contain my glee. Gin DID lie! I was right all along. Ha! "So Gin did have a dog?"

"Well, she must have."

Must have? My excitement dimmed. "Why do you say that? Did you ever meet the dog?"

He shook his head. "No, of course not."

Drat. So much for that. "So why do you think Gin was lying?"

"Because I remember Trisha talking about the dog."

Hold on. Maybe all wasn't lost after all. "Trisha told you about Gin's dog?"

"Yeah, I remember her talking about it when the dog went missing."

"Trisha told you when the dog went missing?"

Nick nodded. "Yeah. She was worried about her aunt. Her uncle died a year or so before, and Gin had taken it really hard. She was all alone in that house, and it wasn't a good situation, so when she got the dog, the rest of the family was relieved. Thought it would do Gin a world of good. Plus, Gin seemed to be a lot happier. Then, when the dog went missing, everyone was understandably worried."

"So then, what happened? Did she regress?"

Nick paused and sipped his coffee. "No, I don't think so. If I recall correctly, Gin was sad about the dog, but it didn't cause a grief relapse like everyone was afraid of."

I waited a beat to see if there was more to the story. "And that's it?"

He raised an eyebrow. "What more were you expecting?"

I wasn't really sure myself. "I don't know. Some reason Gin would want Trisha to lie about it now."

"What, like something happened to the dog, and Gin decided to bury it in the backyard?"

I nearly spit out my too-sweet coffee. "What? What a terrible thing to say."

"Exactly. Which is why Gin might not want anyone to know." His face turned thoughtful as he rubbed his chin. "Although it's not against the law. Not like if, say, a human disappeared and ended up buried in Gin's backyard. That might be a problem."

I pictured Gin cuddling the squirming little Rocky and refused to believe she could possibly have done what Nick was suggesting. "Well, maybe it wasn't Gin after all," I said. "Maybe it was Trisha."

Nick shot me a dubious look. "You think *Trisha* did something to the dog?"

"Of course not," I scoffed. "But what if she was … remembering things wrong?"

"You think Trisha truly doesn't remember if her aunt had a dog or not?"

"No. Not exactly," I said.

"Or you think she's not remembering a dog going missing or not?"

"Look, it's not my idea," I said, feeling huffy.

He gave me an incredulous look. "Then whose idea is it?"

"Well, Mildred seemed to think …"

He held up a hand. "Wait. *Mildred* thinks Trisha doesn't remember if her aunt has a dog or not?"

The more I talked, the more ridiculous I sounded. "Mildred said that when Trisha was younger, she would … ah … have these dreams that were, well …" my voice faded as Nick continued staring at me, his eyes growing wider.

"You think Trisha *dreamed* that her aunt had a dog that went missing?"

"I didn't say that," I said, even though that was precisely what I was saying. "But people do make mistakes sometimes ... like thinking your brother-in-law is dead when he isn't ..."

"Brother-in-law? Whose brother-in-law is dead?"

"No one's. That's the point." I couldn't seem to make myself stop talking, even though Nick was staring at me like I had lost my mind. Maybe I *had* lost my mind. I couldn't even believe the words coming out of my mouth. "Mildred told me about a woman who thought her brother-in-law was dead, but then he showed up at her house and scared her half to death. Maybe this is the same type of thing."

Nick was regarding me with the same look I imagined him giving a wild animal wandering into the coffee shop looking for a latte—like he wasn't exactly sure if I was rabid or not. "So let me get this straight. Some acquaintance of Mildred thought her brother-in-law was dead, even though he wasn't, so therefore, it makes perfect sense that Trisha thought her aunt had a dog go missing, when her aunt never had a dog."

"Something like that," I said weakly. It sounded even stupider when he said it like that. "Okay look, I know it sounds a little far-fetched ..."

Nick raised an eyebrow. "A *little*?"

I ignored him and kept going. "But people make mistakes all the time. Cops will say eyewitnesses of crimes are notoriously bad at remembering details. One person will describe the perpetrator as a tall, thin guy with blonde hair, while the second will say he's short and fat with black hair."

"We're not talking about a crime being committed."

"It's still the same principle," I insisted. "It's possible Trisha might have made a mistake. Right?"

"By that logic, anything is possible," Nick said. "Heck, maybe it isn't about Trisha's memory, after all. Maybe *Gin* forgot she had a dog. Hey, anything is possible, right?"

"Maybe Gin did forget she had a dog," I snapped. "Maybe she had a brain injury or is experiencing early-stage amnesia."

"Or maybe she just doesn't want to talk about her dog," Nick said. "Think about it. Some stranger shows up on her doorstep and asks her a bunch of questions about a painful time in her life. Maybe rather than tell you it's none of your business, she decided to pretend it never happened."

I paused. It never occurred to me that the truth might be too painful for her. Again, I pictured her blanching when I mentioned her "other" dog. Was it grief I had seen in her face? "But you just said the family was relieved because Gin wasn't as upset as they thought she would be about the dog. So, she couldn't have been *that* disturbed. Plus, why would Trisha tell us to investigate if she knew it would be upsetting to Gin?"

"Who knows? Maybe Trisha thought she was helping Gin," Nick said. "But this is all speculation at this point. We won't know anything for sure until we ask Trisha what happened. It's even possible it's me—maybe *I'm* not remembering it right."

"You?" I widened my eyes in mock horror. "It couldn't possibly be *you*. You have a memory like a steel trap, or something like that, I'm sure."

Nick's lips quirked up in amusement. "As much as I appreciate the sentiment, it *was* a year ago, and Trisha and I were ... well, it doesn't matter now."

I squeezed my coffee cup, desperately wanting to ask him exactly what had been going on between him and Trisha. But I also didn't want him to know just how badly I wanted that information. Instead, I took another sip of my coffee, cursing myself yet again for forgetting how sweet it was. *Focus, Emily. This isn't about Nick's relationship with Trisha, but Trisha's relationship with her aunt.* "I guess we'll just have to wait for more information."

"I guess." Nick sipped his coffee, lifting his eyes to meet mine above the rim. I sucked in my breath. I had forgotten how green his eyes were. Like rich emeralds shot with just a hint of gold. And his lashes were so long, they should have been outlawed.

For a moment, we just stared at each other. I was suddenly hyper aware of him—the way his broad chest moved slightly under his button-down shirt, the sleeves rolled up to the elbows and his tie askew. The way his eyes widened ever so slightly, like he was as surprised as I was to be there.

"Um … Emily," he started to say, right as a loud, high-pitched voice screeched right in my ear, "Are you going to hog the sugar?"

I started, turning to see a girl who didn't look old enough to be drinking coffee glaring at me. Her hair was way too black to be natural, paired with way too much black eye makeup and clothing.

"Sorry," I mumbled, stepping out of the way. She rolled her eyes and flounced toward the sugar. A part of me itched to tell her she was going to stunt her growth with that coffee, but I reminded myself it wasn't my business.

"I probably should get back to the office," Nick said, glancing at his watch.

"Yeah, I should too," I said, pushing down the irrational disappointment flooding over me. I was being silly. I absolutely did need to get back to the agency. I could just imagine the chaos that was waiting for me there. For all I knew, Mildred had talked the other two into purchasing something ridiculous, like a rocket launcher, and if I didn't get back in time, I wouldn't be able to stop it.

Not to mention it was better for us to leave anyhow. Nick was with Trisha, after all. And I … well, I didn't know if I had a shot with Jerome, but I had no business being there with Nick. Even if he was the first person who took my concerns about this dog mystery seriously.

He took a step away from me, his eyes not meeting mine. "I guess I'll catch you later, then."

"Um … okay," I said as he strode across the coffee shop toward the front door. I had so many questions I still wanted to ask: Was he going to talk to Trisha? Was he going to tell me what she said? What was going on between them a year ago? What about today?

But as I watched him walk away from me (and tried not to enjoy the view too much), it was clear he was done with the conversation. Even if I wasn't.

That thought was like being splashed with cold water. What was wrong with me? Nick was with another woman, yet there I was, standing in a coffee shop mooning over him like some silly lovestruck schoolgirl. Enough of that nonsense. I strode toward the door, tossing what was left of my too-sweet coffee into the trash. What a waste of a good latte.

I berated myself for the entire walk back to the agency. It was time to be done with Nick, Trisha, mysterious dogs, Jerome, and more. No more messing around. I was going to get myself focused. I didn't need a man. I had plenty of other things going on, not to mention that I was an independent, smart woman who was firmly in control of her life. I was good. More than good. I was perfect.

By the time I reached the agency, I was sticky with sweat and ready to take my life back. Or maybe it was more like I was ready for a challenge. Or … a fight. Whatever it was, I was ready for it.

I swung open the door to hear Mildred say, "… I don't care what you say, give me a revolver any day. Much safer, and you're less likely to have a jam, especially in a pinch."

A revolver? I whirled around to see a different magazine, one I hadn't seen before, spread out over the Aunt Tilde's desk. Even from where I stood across the room, I could see the gleam of the various metals. "What did you just say?"

"Oh, hi Emily. You have a message," Aunt Tilde said, barely glancing up from where Mildred was gesturing. Nora was straining to peer over their shoulders. "It's on your desk."

I didn't move, instead planting my hands on my hips. "That's not what I asked."

"I like that one," Nora said, pointing. "It's kind of cute.

"We don't need 'cute,'" Mildred said.

"But it doesn't hurt," Nora said.

"Just as long as it does the job," Aunt Tilde said.

"What job?" I practically screeched.

Aunt Tilde's eyes flickered up. "Didn't you hear me? You have a message."

"I think this one would be better for our purposes, but we probably should test them all out," Mildred said.

"I don't care about the message," I said, annoyed. "Are you looking at what I think you're looking at?"

"Why? Do you have a recommendation?" Mildred asked.

"If it is what I think it is, then yes. We don't get one," I said.

Aunt Tilde waved at me. "Oh, Emily. How else are we going to protect ourselves on a stakeout if we don't have a weapon?"

"You shouldn't need to protect yourself," I said.

Mildred clucked her tongue. "You're right, we shouldn't. But it's always good to be prepared."

"The detectives on television always have guns," Nora said.

"Those are fictional detectives," I said.

"Yes, but they still need them in the situations they find themselves in. We might, too," Nora said.

"Especially on a stakeout," Mildred said.

I gritted my teeth. "You're taking pictures of a man who may or may not be cheating on his wife. You're not busting a drug ring."

"Not at the moment," Mildred said. "But you never know what opportunities might walk right through that door."

An image of Mildred and Aunt Tilde crashing a drug house, the dealers looking up in surprise as Mildred waved a gun around, nearly shooting Nora—who is holding a container of fresh cookies—in the process flitted through my mind, and I bit my lip to keep from laughing. "You know, you can't just buy a gun," I said. "You have to make sure it's licensed and legal and all of that."

Aunt Tilde waved her hand. "Oh, of course it will be legal. Don't worry about that."

With that answer, I was *absolutely* worried about that.

"You really ought to check your message," Mildred said. "We can show you the models we're considering after that."

I knew I should say something. There had to be something I could say that would inject reason into the conversation. But even as I stood there, my mouth working, I couldn't think of a single word. So instead, I strode over to my desk. With my luck, the message would be from a gun salesman.

But it wasn't. Or any salesman, for that matter.

It was from Jerome.

Chapter 11

"So, how are things going at Aunt Tilde's protection racket company?" Ellen asked.

I made a face into the phone receiver. "It's a detective agency, not a protection racket."

My sister snorted. "Same difference. At least when it comes to Aunt Tilde. You know whatever she's up to is barely on the side of legal. If it even is legal."

"This isn't like her other ventures," I insisted.

"Which is also precisely what Aunt Tilde would say if asked."

"Oh, for Pete's sake, do you really think I would be involved in something shady?" I demanded.

"Of course not," Ellen said. "You're as honest and straightforward as they come." My mouth fell open in surprise. Ellen almost never paid me a compliment. I wondered what it meant. Was it possible our relationship might be on an upswing?

But no. That was wishful thinking on my part, as she unfortunately kept talking. "And Aunt Tilde knows that, too. Which is why I would expect she's kept some of the dirty details to herself."

"What?" I squeaked. "I'm the office manager. She's hired me to run the agency like a proper business." Even as I said it, Aunt Tilde's voice floated through my head. *Emily, you worry too much. Of course it's going to be legal.*

"Just because you're the office manager doesn't mean you know everything that's going on in the business," Ellen said.

"That's actually the definition of being an office manager. You manage the office," I said.

"Mm hmm. Did you ever find out why Aunt Tilde is driving a Mary Kay car?"

Drat. I had almost forgotten about that. "That's different. It's her personal car."

"Of course it's different. Keep telling yourself that."

Ugh. I really needed to rethink these weekly "sisterly" catch-ups. "What's going on with you?"

"Oh, same old, same old." In the background, I could hear my nieces screaming at each other.

"How are my darling nieces?"

"They're fine."

"And Ian?"

"He's fine. Everything's fine." Was it my imagination, or did her voice sound testy? "But stop trying to change the subject. We're not done talking about you. How did your date with Jerome go?"

"Fine." Briefly, I considered telling her about Mildred and Aunt Tilde crashing it, but decided against it.

"Are you going to see him again?"

"Actually, I already have." Jerome had wanted to meet after work for a drink—a "do-over," he'd called it with a laugh. He'd also explained that he would have called sooner, but he had a bit of a family emergency he'd been taking care of.

"I hope everything is okay," I said, and he assured me everything had worked out. His mother had a bad fall late Saturday afternoon, but thankfully, she hadn't broken anything. There was some bad bruising, but she was set to make a full recovery. I was touched he had dropped everything to take care of her like that.

Just like Friday night, we had gone to The Tipsy Cow, but the crowd was quite different. Unlike before, it was filled with professionals grabbing a quick drink—women in stylish suits and men in button-down shirts and ties. For a moment, I could only stand there, wracked with grief and nostalgia. That had been my life, just a few months before: drinks with coworkers, wearing my own smart suits paired with leather pumps and a drop of expensive perfume subtly dabbed behind each ear. Those suits were now buried at the back of my closet, pushed aside so I would see them as little as possible, and I'd left the perfume at my old apartment. Sometimes, Geoff would surprise me and join me, my handsome fiancé impeccably dressed in a power suit. Not like Nick, in his slightly rumpled shirts and tie askew.

Speaking of Nick … oh no. I quickly glanced around, sure I would see him there, probably with Trisha … maybe even asking her about her aunt and what she'd said to me. Oh man, that was the last thing I wanted to interrupt.

But to my relief, there was no Nick in sight. Instead, Jerome had led me to a quiet booth where we both had a single drink.

"You did? Oh, he must really like you," Ellen gushed. "And do you like him?"

"I do." Once it had fully hit me that I was grieving an illusion—one that included having a secure job, a loving relationship, and a bright future—I was able to enjoy my time with Jerome.

"So I'm assuming you're seeing him again?"

"Yes, this Friday."

She squealed, and I quickly moved the phone away from my ear. "See, I told you. I knew you would find someone else. Geoff was a jerk. He didn't deserve you."

Despite not completely believing her, it still felt good to hear her say it.

"Has he kissed you yet?"

"Ellen!" Even though she couldn't see me, I could feel my cheeks growing hot.

"What? It's a natural question."

"If you're in high school," I huffed. "Not at our age."

"What, you think you've outgrown kissing?" she teased.

My face was on fire. I was so glad she couldn't see me. "He's a gentleman. Besides, I don't kiss and tell."

She burst out laughing. "Yeah right. You couldn't wait to tell me about Geoff kissing you." Her voice sobered. "But I'm glad he's a gentleman. You deserve to be treated well, Emily."

For the second time in a week, that tightness I seemed to constantly carry in my chest loosened a little more, and I felt like I might cry.

"So, back to Aunt Tilde and this … whatever it is." Her voice was brisk, as if she too had felt the sudden emotion and wanted to back way up to a respectable distance.

I cleared my throat. "Detective agency."

"Whatever. Do you have any interesting cases?"

"We do, actually. A couple of them. Err … I mean, only one that's official." I winced. Whatever this thing was with Trisha and Gin, it wasn't a case, and I had to stop thinking of it as such.

"You have both an official and an unofficial case? That sounds intriguing."

"It's really not," I said. "A woman came in and wants us to investigate her husband. She thinks he's cheating on her."

"Well, that's depressing … trying to prove someone is a cheater."

"Actually, Aunt Tilde and the other two …" I paused, unsure what to call them. "Detectives" seemed a little too grandiose. "The other two partners are pretty excited about it."

"Why on earth would they be excited about such a horrible situation?"

"Well, they get to go on a stakeout. You know, to try to catch him in the act and take a picture of it. They think it's going to be a lot of fun."

"What do you think?"

Scout ambled up to me, and I bent down to rub his neck. "I think they're going to be bored out of their mind. And then they'll decide maybe they don't like going on stakeouts after all, but it's going to be too late, because the agency has already invested in all sorts of equipment. So, they'll really have to take on a few more of these cases just so the investment pays off."

"Well, you never know. That equipment might come in handy. You might have other cases that are more interesting than trying to track down a cheating husband."

Scout nudged me with his head so I would keep petting him. "Actually, that might be worse. That might be dangerous. At least this guy, who may or may not be cheating on his wife, provides less opportunity for a screwup."

"Wait a minute. You don't believe the wife that her husband is cheating on her?"

It took me a moment to think back to what I had said. I hadn't realized I had actually voiced my doubts out loud. "Honestly, I have no idea. I have no proof either way. I only know what the wife told us."

"But you must know something," Ellen persisted.

I chewed on my bottom lip. "There was just something … off about her. It's hard to explain, but something just didn't feel right about the case."

"But Aunt Tilde took it anyway."

"Stakeout, remember?"

Ellen laughed. "Everyone has their priorities. Okay, so now tell me about the other case. The unofficial one."

I was silent for a moment. Did I really want to go there with Ellen? Everyone else thought I was overreacting, and I assumed she would, too.

Well, everyone but Nick. But that was neither here nor there.

"It's nothing," I said.

"Oh, come now. I'm sure it's not nothing," Ellen said. "You're good at spotting inconsistencies. That's always been one of your superpowers. So, what are the inconsistencies here?"

Again, I was so taken aback by Ellen's compliment—twice in one conversation!—that I found myself telling her the story despite my better judgement.

"That is really weird," Ellen said. "Especially the part where—is her name Trisha?—recanted what she told you."

"I know, right?" Oh my gosh, two people had now shared my disbelief. Maybe I wasn't so crazy after all. "Why would she make a point of telling me she made a mistake? Why not just drop the whole thing?"

"I agree, it makes no sense. So why does Aunt Tilde think this is a non-case?"

"Both Mildred and Aunt Tilde think there's a reasonable explanation."

Ellen sounded legitimately surprised. "A reasonable explanation? Like what? That Gin is just flat out lying to you for some reason?"

"Actually, that's not one of the theories, but it probably should be. No, mostly they think that Trisha made a mistake. Either she's remembering what happened wrong or she dreamed it. Something like that."

Ellen sounded mystified. "Really? How old is Trisha?"

"I'm not sure, but probably close to my age."

"And they think she's remembering it wrong? Does she have a bad memory?"

"I really have no idea. I don't know her very well. Although Nick doesn't seem to think so."

"Nick? Who's Nick?"

Oops. "He's … um … he's that attorney I mentioned who's helping out at the agency. Doing some pro-bono work."

"And he knows Trisha?"

"They're dating."

"Oh. And you asked him about Trisha?" Her voice was heavy with disbelief.

"Well, we are friends." More like associates, I mentally corrected, although it felt too complicated to try to explain to Ellen.

"Friends?"

"Ellen, for goodness' sake, what are you saying? Of course we're friends. He's over at the agency every day."

"The agency needs that much legal work?"

"No, he's been remodeling the kitchen."

"He's doing what? Is he a contractor or an attorney?"

"I guess both. But we're getting off track. The point is, he does know Trisha, and he doesn't think she has any memory issues."

"Okay then. You don't have to bite my head off." I clamped my jaw together to keep the words insisting that I wasn't from spilling out. "Did *Nick* happen to mention if she had any other issues?"

I grimaced, but managed to keep my tone neutral. "No, I don't think so."

"Doesn't that seem a little far-fetched? That someone our age would have problems with their memory?"

"That was my thought, but both of them seem convinced."

"Well, maybe they don't remember what it's like to be our age," Ellen said. "Quite honestly, if someone is having memory issues, I would think it would be more likely to be Gin than Trisha. It's possible there IS something wrong with Gin, but she's refusing to deal with it, so the rest of the family is walking on eggshells around her."

"That certainly makes more sense than Trisha remembering wrong. Although I suppose anything is possible."

"What do you think? Could Gin be suffering from dementia?"

I pictured Gin, standing with a wiggling Rocky in her arms and the look of horror on her face when I mentioned the missing dog. "I suppose it's possible," I said slowly. "But when I asked her about the dog, she didn't look surprised or puzzled, which is how you would think she would look if she had absolutely no idea what I was talking about."

"How did she look?"

I paused. "I guess … scared."

"Scared? Seriously?"

"Yeah, it was strange. The whole thing was strange."

"Not even sad?"

"No, not really." I thought about what Nick said—that maybe Gin was lying because she didn't want to talk to a stranger about her missing dog. But if that were the case, wouldn't she look upset? Or angry, even?

"Scared," Ellen mused. "I wonder what she would have to be scared about. Do you think she did something to the dog?"

"I can't imagine that. Her new dog Rocky looked spoiled rotten."

"Yeah, that doesn't make much sense. If this was a missing human, I would assume she had buried him in the backyard. But it's not against the law to bury a dog, so that's probably not what's going on."

It was on the tip of my tongue to say, "That's what Nick said," but at the last moment, I bit it back. Ellen was suspicious enough about my relationship with Nick. I didn't need to add any more fuel to the fire.

"So, what are you going to do?" Ellen asked.

"About what?"

"What do you mean, about what? This case! What have we been talking about?!"

I moved to the window that overlooked my aunt's garden, staring outside as I started twisting and untwisting the phone cord. "I don't know if there's anything I can do."

"Of course there is. There must be. For heaven's sake, you work at a detective agency. You need to investigate."

Scout thrust his head under my hand again, so I stopped worrying about the phone cord to pet him instead. "But I don't know if there's anything for me to investigate. Both Gin and Trisha say there was no dog, and Aunt Tilde seems to think the case is closed. So, I think it's done."

"It's not done," Ellen scoffed. "Something is going on, and you really need to get to the bottom of it."

"But I don't know if it's any of my business. I mean, isn't this more of a family affair?"

"A family affair? Really? Since when has that ever stopped anyone?" Ellen let out a guffaw. "Seriously, Em. There's something strange going on. If it was just Gin telling you there was no dog, well, then maybe you would be right. Maybe Gin just doesn't want to revisit what happened to her dog with a stranger. But to me, Trisha's reaction is what puts this over the top. For her to ask you to do this and then make a big show of telling you she was mistaken? No, there's something off, and I think you should look into it."

"But how?" Ugh. I sounded like an idiot. Although in my defense, Ellen's words had so floored me, I wasn't sure how to respond.

"I'm sure you'll figure it out," Ellen said confidently.

Chapter 12

I pushed open the doors of the Redemption Public Library, taking a moment to breathe in the familiar scents of paper, leather, and soft, comfy cushions. One of my favorite places to go as a child was the library. I would spend hours curled up in a beanbag in the children's section, devouring every book I could get my hands on. It was so much better that being in my house. Home was never safe. I was constantly walking on eggshells, my stomach a mess of knots, always trying to stay on my mother's good side while she drowned herself in a bottle. That was never the case at the library.

For a moment, I considered abandoning the task in front of me to spend the afternoon finding a few good books to read, but I reminded myself I had a job to do. Never mind that it would likely go nowhere. I still owed it to myself to at least try.

"Do you have copies of *The Redemption Times*?" I asked the woman behind the counter. She looked like a bundle of contradictions, with her long, reddish-brown hair plaited in two messy braids, total lack of make-up, and tiny gold stud in her nose. She was also dressed in jeans, a white shirt, and a thick brown cardigan, even though it was over eighty outside and she couldn't be much older than me. Although, to be fair, the air conditioning was cranked up to nearly arctic temperatures.

She pushed her gold-rimmed glasses up on her nose (which is when I realized they matched the gold stud in her nose) and peered at me. "Yes, we have a subscription. Are you looking for today's paper? I think that man is still reading it." She pointed at an older, balding man, who was also dressed in layers sitting at one of the long tables.

"Actually, I was hoping to look at last year's."

She slid off the stool she was perched on. I noticed she had a small, gold nametag attached to her sweater with the name Vivian written on it. "Oh, if that's the case, let me show you where we keep them." She started to lead me through the library. "How far back do you want to go?"

"Just a year."

She stopped in front of a large wooden shelf that had stacks of newspapers in labeled boxes. "Do you have a specific date you're looking for?"

"No, I'm not really sure. I just know it's around a year ago."

She nodded distractedly, as she quickly scanned the different dates. "Okay, so last year's papers start here." She tapped one of the boxes. "Each box should have about two weeks of papers in it. You can see the dates here." She pointed at the printed label on the side. "If you need to go back further, just keep going backwards. If it's past five years, you'll need to switch to microfilm. I can help you with the machine if you need it."

"Oh, no I shouldn't have to go that far back," I said, staring at the boxes of newspapers. There were so many of them, especially since I had no idea where to even begin looking. Should I take Trisha literally and start with a year ago today? Or did she mean it more loosely, like any time last year?

This was going to take me hours, especially since I wasn't even sure what I was looking for. Maybe this wasn't such a good idea after all.

The woman must have seen something in my face, because her expression softened. "Do you want to tell me what you're looking for? I might be able to help."

I half-smiled. "How about a missing dog?" My tone was joking, as I didn't really expect any help, but hey, it couldn't hurt. Growing up, I had been amazed at the obscure pieces of information librarians were able to track down.

She cocked her head, her expression serious. "I would check the classifieds."

I looked at her in surprise. "People put missing dogs in the classifieds section?" It never occurred to me to check there, although to be honest, I had only ever read that section when I was actively looking for a job.

She nodded. "Oh yes. You'd be surprised by what you can find in the classifieds. I would start in the lost and found, but sometimes, people place larger ads for a lost pet. I've even occasionally seen the paper do an article about missing pets, but that's usually when there's been a rash of disappearances, which does happen from time to time. It is Redemption, after all." She gave me a considering look. "Is that what happened a year ago? Was there another rash of pet disappearances?"

Her question took me by surprise. Was that what had happened? But why hadn't anyone else said anything? "I'm actually not sure. Do you remember anything out of the ordinary?"

She shook her head. "But to be honest, I try hard not to remember those times, as they upset me too much. It's tough enough living in this town as it is."

"What do you mean?"

She looked at me in surprise. "Oh, you must be new here. Redemption is the capital of missing people in Wisconsin. I don't know if that's an official title or not, but it probably should be. More people go missing here than anywhere else in the state, despite being a relatively small town. But it's not just disappearances. There are a lot of strange and unusual things that happen here."

"I guess I did know that," I said, although I hadn't considered that Redemption's troubling history might have something to do with a missing dog. "It's because of what happened in the 1880s, right?"

Vivian nodded. "At least, that's what everyone believes. So you've heard the story, then?"

"I have." It was during the blizzard of 1888. One day, all the adults went missing, leaving only the children behind. No one knew what happened, including the children, who swore they never saw anything. But ever since, Redemption had been plagued by bizarre and unexplainable events, including way more disappearances than a town the size of Redemption should have.

"Then you know. I don't know if the town's history was behind your dog going missing, as unfortunately, dogs go missing everywhere in the country. It's not that unusual, but it's certainly possible."

"Actually, it's not my dog, but a … friend's." "Friend" was probably overstating our relationship, but "aunt of the girlfriend of the attorney who does pro-bono work for the detective agency I work at" seemed like TMI.

Vivian's expression was sympathetic. "That's rough. I'm sorry for your friend's loss. Hopefully, you'll find something that will help."

"Thanks," I said, eyeing the boxes. Considering I still wasn't even sure what I was looking for, where to start, or even what I was doing there, finding anything that might help felt pretty impossible.

Except … the Redemption angle had me intrigued. Could it be possible that the town's haunted history had something to do with Gin's missing dog?

Vivian was watching me. "I need to get back to the desk, but I'm happy to help if I can. I'm Vi, by the way. Only my mother calls me Vivian." She grinned as she gestured toward her nametag. I couldn't help but grin back.

"Emily. And thanks."

Once Vi left, I stared at the boxes, trying to decide which one to grab first. Should I start at the beginning of the year? January 1992? Or a year ago now, which would be August? I dithered for a while, listing pros and cons in my head before finally grabbing the box for the first part of June 1992. It seemed to me that even if Trisha didn't remember an exact date, around a year ago was a good place to start, as it would have been summer. I could at least start there, then expand the search if that didn't work.

It took longer than I thought, paging through each individual newspaper. At first, I was only going to look at the classifieds, but Vi's words kept ringing in my head. If something else had been going on a year ago, something other than leaving a gate open or a dog slipping a lead, it was possible someone turned it into a story. The only way I would find it was if I skimmed the entire paper. And that took time.

It didn't take long for me to realize what I had feared—that pretty much none of the stories were applicable. Even what I found in the classified ads around missing pets wasn't helpful (although Vi was right that there were a lot of them, unfortunately). Most of the articles were about city council meetings, PSAs about not leaving your kids unattended near swimming pools or in locked in cars, and notices about local bake sales and carwashes. But there *were* a disturbing number of articles around people who had gone missing. Even though I wasn't looking for a missing person, I still found myself reading them. The elderly father who insisted he was fine living alone hadn't been seen in three days. The twenty-year-old who stopped showing up for work one day and hadn't been seen since. The mother who wasn't home when her children got back from school. All of that worry, the unknowing, the heartbreak. I couldn't stop reading even though I knew I was wasting my time.

In addition to the missing person articles, there was also a weekly column that summarized all the police activity for the week. Most of the arrests were fairly minor, like shoplifting and vandalism, but two were more serious. A Peeping Tom had been arrested after a half-dozen women had complained, and another pervert had been arrested after exposing himself to a woman jogging in the park. Ugh. Even in a small town like Redemption, you couldn't get away from the freaks.

"How is it going?" Vi had returned and was standing near the table. I glanced at the clock and saw it was close to one. I had been there for nearly three hours. The library appeared to be empty; even the old man who had been reading the paper had disappeared.

"Fine," I said, leaning back to stretch the kink in my neck. "Slow."

She smiled. "I can imagine. Any luck finding anything?"

"Well, you're right about the classifieds. I did find notices for pets, both from people who found stray animals and some who had lost theirs," I said.

She was studying my face. "But not your friend's."

I sighed. "Not yet."

She gave me a sympathetic look. "I would imagine it's kind of like looking for a needle in a haystack, when you don't know the exact date or what you're even looking for."

I grimaced. She wasn't wrong. "Something like that."

She nodded and started straightening the papers even though they were perfectly straight. "I know it's none of my business, but I am a little curious. What are you hoping to find? Is there some reason why your friend doesn't know what happened to her dog? Was someone else taking care of the animal, or does she have amnesia?" She gave me a self-conscious smile. "Sorry, I read too many detective books. It just seems a little odd to be searching the papers for a dog that went missing a year ago."

Ugh. This was why I hadn't wanted to tell anyone why I was there. How could I explain what I was doing? It made no sense, even to myself.

Unless … I told the truth. Or at least a partial truth.

I took a deep breath. "Well, I wasn't exactly honest with you. My friend isn't the person who lost the dog. It's her aunt. And … well, it's kind of a long story, but her aunt denied she even had a dog, and my … my friend is not being straight about it either. First, she said her aunt did have a dog, and now she's saying no, she was mistaken, and her aunt didn't have a dog. So the whole thing is just … odd."

I glanced at Vi's face, sure I would see her staring at me like I had lost my mind, but instead, she was giving me a knowing look. "And you thought you'd do a little research to see if you could discover the truth."

"Exactly." Wow, first my sister and now Vi, the librarian. Finally, I was finding people who understood me.

She gave me a secretive smile. "I totally get it. I would be doing the same thing."

"Right? It's weird, isn't it? Why would you say your aunt had a dog that went missing a year ago, and then backtrack and say you were mistaken? Who makes that mistake?"

She pressed a finger against her lips. "Okay, so let's start from the beginning. Why did your friend tell you about her aunt's missing dog in the first place?"

"Um, well …" It was a good question, and not one I wanted to answer. But if Vi was going to help me, I didn't have much of a choice. "I think it was because she thought I could help."

She stared at me blankly. "Help? How?"

I swallowed. "I actually work at a detective agency, so I think she thought I could help find her aunt's dog."

Vi's eyes lit up. "Really? Which one?"

"Um, The Redemption Detective Agency."

"Is that Tilde Tillerson's new agency?"

I blinked. How could she possibly know that? "Yeah, actually, it is."

Vi bobbed her head up and down. "Cool. Tilde is great."

"Yeah, she is," I said weakly.

"So, okay." Vi held up her hand and started using her fingers to tick off each point she made. "Your friend tells you her aunt's dog is missing, presumably so you can find it. Which means she thinks the dog is alive. So why would she think that?"

"Because the dog ran away?" I guessed.

Vi nodded. "That's one reason, sure. So, unless the dog is still wandering around Redemption as a stray, he probably got adopted by a family somewhere. Which isn't impossible to track down, but it's certainly not easy."

"No, that wouldn't be easy." I sat back in my chair, crossing my arms over my chest. "You said one reason. What other reason do you think there might be? Do you think someone dognapped her aunt's dog?"

A grin tugged on the corner of her mouth. "So, hear me out before you think I'm crazy."

I sat up straight. "By who? And why?"

Vi held up a hand. "Hold on. Just hear me out. I was remembering something earlier, and … well, it is a little nuts, but it kind of fits, too. About a year ago, a dog walker went missing."

My jaw dropped. "A dog walker? Someone who was walking their own dog went missing? Or was this like a professional dog walker?"

"Like a professional dog walker, except to be fair, he did more than just walk dogs. He was also a trainer, and I think he did some boarding. I don't remember all the details, but I remember the story, because I had a friend who used him for dog training, and she was really worried when he disappeared."

"So, what happened to him?"

She spread her arms out. "No one knows. As far as I know, he wasn't ever located."

Something shifted in my gut, and I started to reach for the newspapers. "And this was a year ago, you said?" It didn't make any sense.

It couldn't possibly be related to what happened to Gin's dog, but my gut was screaming otherwise.

She nodded. "Yeah, it was sometime last summer. I remember that, although I don't remember the date."

"Was it in the paper?"

"It was. That's how my friend found out about it. Part of the never-ending Missing People series."

I started thumbing through the paper in front of me. "What about the police? Did they investigate?"

She shrugged. "I doubt it."

"What do you mean?"

"Well, first off, if the police tried to investigate every missing person's case, they wouldn't be able to get anything else done. You saw the articles. There are just way too many disappearances for law enforcement to handle. But besides that, it's not against the law for an adult to go missing. A child, yes. The cops will usually get involved with those cases pretty fast. And if it appears that the adult didn't go willingly or something happened to them, then they'll investigate. But if an adult disappears, and there's no evidence of foul play ..." She held up her hands in a helpless gesture.

"Is that why they write up the disappearances in the paper, then? To try to help?"

"Probably. That was what I always figured. Try to do whatever you can, even if it's not much."

I looked down at the paper and thought about the stories I had already read. The mother, the twenty-year-old, the elderly father. So much pain. I wondered if any of them ever had a happy ending.

"Anyway," Vi said briskly, brushing her hands down her jeans as if trying to wipe away the unpleasantness. "I have no idea if that missing dog walker disappeared with a dog or even knew your friend's aunt, but I thought it might be a lead. A place to start. And if not him, maybe someone else took your friend's dog. It's worth looking into, I think."

I looked down at the paper again. "I think you might be on to something."

Chapter 13

For the second time in a little over a week, I found myself at the bottom of the driveway, staring at the neat blue and white ranch house. Again, I wondered how I managed to get myself into these situations. The old Emily, the one who lived in Riverview and wore trendy and uncomfortable suits to a modern office, would never find herself in such a ridiculous situation, harassing a stranger about a dog they claimed never existed.

But there I was. Again. Except this time, I had reinforcements, so to speak.

I found the article in August's paper, almost exactly a year ago, although when the disappearance actually happened was up for debate.

His name was Ed Wheeler. He was apparently retired but had a side business working with dogs as a walker, trainer, and sitter. He was last seen by one of his clients one warm, sunny morning, walking a well-behaved German shepherd. She was weeding in her front yard and waved at him. He waved back and kept walking. She had seen him walking the shepherd in the past and assumed it was one of his dog-walking clients, as she knew he lived in a small apartment and didn't have one of his own. But she didn't know whose dog it was.

That was the last time anyone had seen him, although it was at least a few days (if not longer) before he was reported missing. When he didn't show up to his dog-training class, one of his students went to his apartment building and got his landlord involved. When they unlocked his door, it appeared like Ed had left for a few days. The apartment was mostly clean, but there was a layer of dust blanketing the surfaces. There was still food in the fridge and clothes hanging in his closet, though, and his toothbrush was still in the bathroom. The only things that appeared to be missing were his wallet and his car. Everything else seemed to be accounted for.

They called the cops, because it wasn't like Ed to not show up to class, but they weren't able to do much. There was no sign of foul play, and other than the fact that none of Ed's clients had heard from him, there was no reason to suspect he was even missing. It was more likely he had gone out of town for a few days. But why didn't he tell anyone? Perhaps it was an emergency, the cops had pontificated. Chances were high that Ed would reappear at some point with a reasonable explanation.

Several weeks passed with no sign of Ed. None of his bills were paid, including his rent. This time, the cops did file a report, with the caveat there was little they could do. "It's not against the law for an adult to disappear."

At this point, the newspaper was alerted, and the reporter did a little investigating into the story, including speaking to the woman who may have been the last person to see Ed. The reporter also included the street Ed was last seen on. After consulting a map of Redemption, which Vi had so helpfully provided me, I discovered it was only a few blocks away from where Gin lived.

While it certainly didn't prove anything, it was … curious. It definitely warranted a second conversation.

Before I lost my nerve, I strode up to the front the door and rang the bell. I waited, listening carefully, but could hear nothing. No sounds of little dog toenails clicking against the floor, no barking, no echoes of adult footsteps.

I rang the doorbell again, even though I figured it was futile. Maybe I should have called first, though I was unsure whether Gin would actually meet with me if given the choice. Especially when I told her what it was about.

Sighing, I turned to head back to my car. Maybe I would just have to keep coming by until I got lucky and found her at home. It wasn't a great plan, but it was the only one I had.

"She's not home."

A woman was crouched down next to a flower garden that edged the house next door. She was probably in her late sixties or early seventies and wore a floppy, bright-pink hat, a cheery yellow top, bright-green gardening gloves, purple shorts, and overly large sun-glasses. Briefly, I wondered if she and Aunt Tilde were twins sepa-rated at birth. I also wondered how I could have possibly missed her when I came up the front walk. I must have been so focused on my anticipated conversation with Gin that I didn't see her. Because oth-erwise … no, she couldn't have snuck out there while I was standing by Gin's front door. Right?

"Oh, do you know when she'll be back?"

The woman rubbed the sweat away from her forehead, leaving a streak of dirt before standing up, her hand on her back. "Probably be late. Today is the day she volunteers at the Redemption Nursing Home and then hosts Bingo night at her church. She's usually not home until after nine."

Wow, I didn't expect that much detail about Gin's schedule. Es-pecially since this woman didn't know me from Adam. I didn't know how much I would like my neighbor telling anyone who stopped by the details of my daily activity.

Oh, who was I kidding? I had Aunt Tilde and Mildred, who were happy to share the minutia of my life.

"What about tomorrow? Do you think she'll be around then?"

The woman paused and rubbed her chin. "Probably late after-noon. Tomorrow, she usually runs errands after having lunch with friends, but if you come by after that, she should be around. What were you needing, if you don't mind my asking? I may be able to help. I noticed you were here last week."

Of course she did. In my mind's eye, I saw again the curtain flut-tering as I left the first time. I had a feeling then that someone was listening in. Apparently, I had been right.

All that aside, it was possible the neighbor would be more open about this dog business than Gin, so maybe the whole encounter was a blessing in disguise.

"Well, it's kind of a long story," I began.

Even though I couldn't see her eyes behind the round sunglasses, I could almost feel how they sharpened with interest. "I've got a little time. And I'm always happy to be of help."

I bet you are. "Well, to start with, I know Gin's niece, Trisha."

"Of course. Such a lovely girl."

"Yes, well," I stuttered while making a mental note that Trisha had obviously visited Gin enough for the nosy neighbor to know who she was. "Trisha asked me if I could help locate Gin's dog."

Nosy Neighbor's mouth dropped open as she let out a gasp. "Rocky? But I was sure I saw him with Gin when she left today."

"No, not Rocky. The dog before Rocky."

Nosy Neighbor's face shifted to a knowing look. "Ohhh. That dog."

"So there was a dog?"

I didn't mean to sound so desperate, but Nosy Neighbor didn't seem to notice. She was busy shaking her head. "Yes, I know exactly what you're talking about."

"So she did have a dog."

Nosy Neighbor gave me an incredulous look. "Of course she did. Isn't that why you're here?"

I took a chance. "It was a German shepherd, wasn't it?"

She clasped her hands together. "Just the sweetest dog! Rex. I know people say German shepherds can be high strung or whatever, but not Rex. He was such a good dog. And protective, as well. I always felt so safe when he was around."

I couldn't believe my luck. Finally, I had confirmation that there *was* something fishy going on. This was working out better than I had dreamed. "Do you know what happened to him? How he went missing?"

Nosy Neighbor shook her head sadly. "I don't know. I wish I did."

"Weren't you here?" The words were out of my mouth before my brain caught up. Ugh. That wasn't what I meant to say. I sounded like I was blaming her.

But she didn't seem to take it like that. If anything, she looked so disgusted, I thought she might have been secretly blaming herself. "No, but I should have been. I had a doctor's appointment the day he went missing." She clucked her tongue disapprovingly. "I ended up being gone all day. The doctor was running late, and then he wanted me to get some blood drawn, and the lab was running late. I was exhausted when I got home."

"Oh, that sounds awful," I said sympathetically. "I hate it when the doctor is running late."

"Just completely messed up my entire day," Nosy Neighbor said, wiping her forehead again and smearing the dirt even more before removing her gardening gloves. "Would you like some fresh lemonade? I have some in the fridge. I can just run in and grab us a couple of glasses. I'm Blythe, by the way."

"I'm Emily. Nice to meet you. And sure, a glass of lemonade would be lovely."

She waved toward the front of her house. "Why not come sit on the porch, and I'll run in and fetch us both a glass?"

The porch stretched out across the entire front of the house, and in the corner opposite from the front door was a little sitting area with a glass and metal table and two metal chairs. I picked my way around the pots of colorful geraniums and marigolds as Blythe emerged from the house in record time, holding two tall glasses filled with ice and lemonade.

"Thanks," I said, accepting one and taking a sip. It was very cold and a little too sour for my taste, but I smiled and drank more anyway. If Blythe helped me crack this case, I would happily drink a gallon. "So, by the time you got home from the doctor's appointment from hell, Rex had already disappeared?"

She took a drank, shaking her head as she did. "No, I didn't realize Rex was gone until a couple of days later. Gin was gone when I got home. I think she was out looking for the dog, and I barely saw her the following day, either. She was up and out of the house early. I didn't see Rex but thought maybe she had let him out early, and I'd missed him. It wasn't until the day after when I saw her in her backyard with no Rex that she told me he had gone missing."

"Did she tell you what happened?"

Blythe took off her sunglasses and rubbed her eyes. She still had the smudge on her forehead, and now, another along the side of her cheek. With her sunglasses off, she looked older, frailer, the skin papery thin around her temples, and I suddenly felt a burst of sadness for her, spending her days watching her neighbors like a hawk. She must be lonely, and maybe even a little bored. I also felt a little more charitable to Mildred and Aunt Tilde. No wonder why they were both so excited about The Redemption Detective Agency. They needed a way to channel their inner busybody-ness.

"Gin told me the gate hadn't been closed properly, and Rex had gotten out. She said she spent all day searching for him, but no luck. He seemed to have vanished." She took another drink, pursing her lips. "I always thought there was more to the story, and seeing you here, I guess I was right."

I leaned forward slightly, trying to contain my excitement. "Why do you say that?"

"Because Rex was such a good dog. He wouldn't have run away. I know he wouldn't have."

"Did you ever say anything to Gin about it?"

"I tried, but after that first day, Gin didn't want to talk about him anymore. Said it was too painful. She just needed to move on."

That sounded a little like what Nick had said—that maybe Gin was lying because the grief was too much to bear after her husband's death, and she especially didn't want to talk about it with a stranger. Was it possible that was the answer all along?

"But you had your doubts?"

"He was such a good dog," Blythe said again. "I just can't see him running away. Especially with all the training he had."

My ears perked up. Actually, it wasn't just my ears, but every part of my body. I had to remind myself not to seem too eager. "He was trained?"

"Oh my goodness, yes. When Gin first brought Rex home, he was just the cutest little puppy. And she adored him, but she was a little nervous, as well. She had never had a dog before, much less a dog as powerful as a German shepherd. She had wanted a big dog for protection, she said. She'd had a bit of a scare, you see. After her husband died, she was having trouble sleeping, so she began hiking in the woods. Alone, which I didn't think was a smart idea, but she kept telling me she was fine … that she liked the silence. But then something happened on one of her outings, and that was the end of hiking. She would still walk around the neighborhood, but she said she still didn't feel completely safe. So, she decided to get a dog."

"Oh my gosh, what happened to her?"

Blythe sighed and rubbed her forehead. "I think a couple of guys harassed her, but I'm not really sure."

I stared at Blythe. "She didn't tell you?"

Blythe put her lemonade down on the glass table. I could see the condensation dripping down the sides and pooling on the table. "I was here on the porch having a lemonade when Gin came home. It was a hot day; I remember it well because I had spent the afternoon weeding. Gin pulled up in her car. That was the first thing I noticed, because she was driving really erratically. She almost hit the side of the garage. I thought maybe she was having a heart attack or a stroke, so I hurried over to her. She was just sitting there, white as a sheet. I tried to open the door, but it was locked, so I started tapping on the window. I was ready to call an ambulance, but she finally opened the door for me and told me, no, she was fine, she didn't need to go to the hospital. Fine, my foot. She was shaking like a leaf. I got her out of the car and over to my porch and poured her some lemonade. It took a few minutes before she calmed down enough to talk, but even then, she didn't get into a lot of detail. Just that two guys had started harassing her on the path. She had been afraid for her life, but managed to get away. I told her we should call the cops, but she refused. Said they didn't do anything to her, so there was nothing for the cops to do. I said what are you talking about? You were afraid for your life, and that should be a crime right there. But she just repeated that they didn't actually do anything to her. The threat was implied. And they did, in the end, let her go without hurting her, so what *would* be the crime? I said the police could at least talk to them, tell them to leave her alone, if not arrest them for intimidation, or something. She said that could easily backfire. What if they got mad she told the cops about them and decided to go after her again, but this time for real? No, all she wanted to do was forget about it and hope they forgot about her, as well.

"I really thought that was a mistake, but once Gin made up her mind, that was it. There was no talking her out of it. So, when she decided to get a dog, I encouraged her. At least with a dog, especially a nice guard dog like a German shepherd, she'd have some protection."

"So, who did she use for dog training? Do you know?"

Blythe shook her head. "She just said it was someone who specialized in training guard dogs. The way she talked, I thought it might have been someone who lived in Riverview or who wasn't local, and that's why she didn't tell me who it was. It wouldn't be anyone I knew. Not that I knew a lot of dog trainers anyway."

Ed definitely lived locally, so if she was going to Riverview for training, she probably hadn't used him. Of course, she still could have known Ed, even if she wasn't training with him. Or he could have been her trainer, and Gin had decided not to tell her nosy neighbor about him.

But if she did know him, whether he was her trainer or not, why would he kidnap her dog? And why wouldn't she tell anyone if that's what he did? Why would she keep it a secret?

Blythe rattled her lemonade glass, clinking the ice together. "The whole thing just never made sense to me," she said, dropping her voice like she didn't want to be overheard, even though as far as I could see, there was no one around. "I know Gin holds her cards close to her chest, but she loved that dog. Just loved him. She would take him everywhere, and it was obvious that he made her feel so much safer. So if he truly ran off because she left the gate open, why would she stop looking for him after a day? It makes no sense."

I lowered my voice as well. "What do you think happened to Rex?"

She glanced around, as if expecting Gin to pop out of the neighboring rose bushes. "Honestly? I think something happened to him. Like he did get out of the yard because the gate was open and got hit by a car, or something, and she feels so guilty about it that she doesn't want to think about it anymore."

I was loath to admit it, but that did make a certain amount of sense. If her beloved dog had been killed, and it was her fault, I could see her never wanting to talk or think about it again.

"That would also explain why she got that silly rodent of a dog." Blythe pressed her lips together in disapproval. "She didn't want any reminders of her beautiful Rex."

"She certainly did go in the opposite direction with Rocky," I said.

Blythe rolled her eyes. "Never been a fan of little dogs. All they do is yap and yap, although I will admit Rocky isn't as bad as a lot of them. I still wish she had gotten another shepherd, though. Unless …" her voice trailed off, and she pressed her lips together again, shaking her head.

"Unless what?"

She glanced around furtively again. "I probably shouldn't say." She picked up her lemonade and took a long drink.

I leaned forward and kept my voice low. "Say what?"

She shook her head again. "Honestly, it seems a little … fanciful, I know. Poor Rex getting hit by a car seems far more likely, as sad as that would be. But if that is what happened, why is there no blood on his collar?"

For a moment, I could only stare at her, sure I had heard her wrong. "Collar? Rex's collar?"

"Of course." Blythe looked a little put out. "Who else? Certainly not that silly little ball of fluffy nonsense."

"But … I don't understand. How does Gin even have Rex's collar if he ran off?"

Blythe pointed at me. "That's precisely what I'm talking about!"

This was getting stranger and stranger. "How do you know Gin has his collar?"

"Because I saw it. She has a little shrine set up on her mantle." She nodded toward Gin's house. "I saw it a few months after Rex disappeared. There's a picture of Rex, a candle, and his collar. It's very sweet. I didn't say anything at the time, because I knew she didn't want to talk about it, but it kept bothering me, for some reason. And then I realized what it was. There was no blood on his collar. If he had gotten hit by a car, wouldn't there be blood?"

Not necessarily, but I wasn't about to go down that rabbit hole with Blythe. I was more interested in why Gin had a collar from a dog that she claims ran away. "But again, how did she get his collar? Did she take it off of him when he was inside the house?"

"I don't think so. I never saw him without it," Blythe said firmly. "If he was outside, he had his collar on. Period."

As convinced as Blythe sounded, it wasn't exactly proof of any-thing. Gin still could have taken Rex's collar off, and then he went missing. But then I started thinking about the rest of her comments, and I realized it didn't all add up. "Wait, I'm not following you. You think because you saw the collar, he didn't get hit by a car after all?"

"Well, like I said, wouldn't there be something on his collar if he had?" She looked at me like this was completely obvious, and I must be slow.

"Okay, but if he didn't get hit, and he didn't run away, then what happened to him?"

She leaned closer to me. "I think he was dognapped."

My jaw fell open. Had she read my mind? "Dognapped?"

She nodded solemnly. "By those men who harassed her."

My mind went blank, and it took me a minute to connect the dots. "You mean … the men from that hike? The reason she got Rex in the first place?"

She nodded again. "I think they found her and decided to steal Rex."

"Why would they do that?"

She looked surprised. "To torture her some more. Why else?"

That felt like a bit of a stretch. Although the entire conversation was feeling that way. "But that theory begs the same question: if Rex was taken, how did Gin get his collar?"

"Well, clearly, they took it off him first. Probably in front of her while they were still in the yard. They wouldn't want any proof that Rex was her dog, after all."

The notion that two men who had harassed a woman while hiking, found her months or maybe even years later, took her dog out of her yard in front of her, and even took the time to remove his collar and give it to Gin was so ludicrous, I wasn't even sure how to respond. "But I thought you said Rex was a trained attack dog. Wouldn't he have attacked the men?"

"Not if they had a gun," she said.

A gun? Seriously? Oh geez. But honestly, as crazy as this was all sounding, was it really any nuttier than what I'd heard at The Redemption Detective Agency on a daily basis?

"It makes so much sense," Blythe insisted. "Gin never wanted to talk about what happened. Understandable, as she wouldn't want them coming back again. It also explains why her next dog is a little nothing of a thing. Nobody would think that guinea pig a threat, so no one would bother taking it. You see?"

She was looking at me so expectantly, but I was at an absolute loss as to how to respond. "Um ..."

"I should have been home," she said, shaking her head. "If I had been home, I'm sure none of this would have happened. They never would have taken Rex if they knew there was another witness."

She looked so distressed that her doctor's appointment had prevented her from stopping this completely unrealistic fantasy that I found myself patting her hand and consoling her. "Don't blame yourself. You did everything you could."

Chapter 14

"I *told* you to stay in the car," Mildred was saying as she, Aunt Tilde, Nora, and Smoke walked into the agency. It was the middle of the afternoon, and I had been wondering where everyone was. Well, everyone other than me, Scout, and Sherlock, that is. Aunt Tilde had asked me if I would mind bringing the cat in, so we were all there just waiting for everyone else to show up. I had found myself watching the clock as the day ticked by, more eager than I had realized to share what I had learned.

"It's not my fault we needed a bathroom break," Nora said.

"Your bathroom break could have cost us this whole case," Mildred grumbled.

"What happened?" I asked.

"Smoke blew our cover," Mildred said.

I blinked before turning my gaze on the gray cat slinking around Nora's ankles. "Smoke? As in … the cat?"

"Smoke didn't do anything wrong," Nora said. "He just had to go potty. It's not like I could bring his litter box with us."

"I told you not to bring him at all," Mildred said. "A cat has no business on a stakeout."

"But he gets lonely if I leave him at home," Nora cried. Smoke, for his part, sat down and started to clean himself. "Besides, he's good at investigating. He could have helped."

"Helped?" Mildred yelped. "How was he going to help? By bringing us a dead mouse as a gift?"

"It was a squirrel, not a mouse," Nora said. "And he only did that once. Well, twice, but the second time was a mistake."

"How does a cat make a 'mistake' when bringing you a dead animal?" I asked.

"Well, it was still alive," Nora said. "And then it bit me when I was trying to set it free … drew blood and everything. I thought I was going to have to get a rabies shot. It was a huge mess, let me tell you."

"Definitely a mistake," Aunt Tilde said as Smoke continued to lick his paw, totally oblivious to being the center of the conversation. "Smoke would never hurt you. At least not on purpose."

"No, he wouldn't," Nora said. "He's a good cat. He just doesn't understand how sharp his claws are. Or his teeth."

"Maybe he doesn't mean to hurt you, but he certainly did just now," Mildred said. "If that client fires us, it's all his fault."

"I still don't understand what Smoke did," I said.

"He tried to kill the husband," Mildred said. "Darn near succeeded, too."

"Wait, what?" I asked as visions of a lawsuit started dancing in my brain. "Are we still talking about the cat?"

"Who else would we be talking about?" Mildred asked.

"I don't think that's completely fair," Aunt Tilde said, picking up Sherlock and stroking her. "It's not Smoke's fault that the husband nearly tripped over him. Or that he was allergic to him."

"The point is, the cat had no business being there in the first place," Mildred said.

I had to admit, in this case, I completely agreed with Mildred. "Is the husband okay?"

"He's fine," Aunt Tilde said. "Maybe a few bruises, but no worse for wear. I think Smoke broke his fall."

"See? I told you he was just trying to help," Nora said.

I was still stuck on the falling part. "So he actually fell down?"

"He's fine," Aunt Tilde said again. "Nora helped him up and apologized to him, and he told her not to worry about it."

I looked at Nora. "He said that?"

"Something like that," Nora said. "He was sneezing a lot, so it was hard to tell, but I'm sure that's what he meant. He was very nice. Was very interested in learning more about The Redemption Detective Agency."

My mouth dropped. "You told him who you were?"

"Well, of course I did. It would have been rude not to," Nora said. "Plus, it's good promotion. He might become a client."

"The only bad PR is no PR," Aunt Tilde said.

I dropped my head into my hands.

"We better hope he does become a client, as we surely just lost his wife as a client," Mildred said darkly.

I was almost afraid to ask. I picked up my head to peer through my fingers at her and braced myself. "Is there anything else I should know?"

"We didn't get any photos," Mildred said. "Not a single one."

"Why not?" I asked. "Because of Smoke?"

"Smoke had nothing to do with it," Nora said.

"That's not exactly true, Mildred," Aunt Tilde said. "We did get photos."

"Not the right ones," Mildred said darkly.

"That's not true either," Nora said. "We got some lovely pictures. I got a great one of an owl perched in this old oak tree. And Tilde got some nice ones, too."

"Especially the ones of the sunset," Aunt Tilde said. "Those were my favorite."

"But what about the husband?" I asked. I had a sudden image in my head of Jan sitting in the office, staring at a photo of a squirrel, or maybe Smoke, a look of utter bewilderment on her face while Nora tried to explain the different shots to her.

"Oh, he's fine," Aunt Tilde said, flapping her hands. "And I almost forgot to tell you, Emily, your client was there."

"My client?" I stared at her bewilderedly. "What client?"

"You know, what's-her-name? Trisha's aunt," Aunt Tilde said.

"Gin? But she's not exactly a client," I said.

"Close enough," Aunt Tilde said.

"Yes, but…Wait a minute," I gave Aunt Tilde a hard look. "Were you taking pictures of Gin?"

"Taking pictures of Gin? Why would we do that?" Mildred asked, looking at Aunt Tilde. "She wasn't part of the stakeout."

"Don't you remember? We saw Gin," Aunt Tilde said. "At the grocery store."

"Oh, that's right. It *was* kind of suspicious, now that you mention it," Mildred said.

"Um …" *Dare I even ask?* "What's suspicious about Gin going to the grocery store?"

"She bought a lot of groceries," Mildred said.

I looked between the three of them. "Gin bought … groceries? At the grocery store …"

"Not just groceries," Aunt Tilde corrected. "A *lot* of groceries. Too many. Especially for a single woman."

I was at a loss. "Maybe she's shopping for a party. Or maybe she only shops once a month."

"No, she wasn't shopping for a party," Mildred said decisively.

"How would you know?" I asked her. "Did you see what was in her bags?"

"Because she would be buying things like cases of soda and potato chips," Mildred said. "Party food. There was no party food."

"Okay, so maybe she only shops once a month, so it's obviously a bigger haul," I said.

Aunt Tilde shook her head. "You don't understand. It wasn't what a woman would generally buy."

I stared at her. "I'm sorry? Men and woman buy different things?"

"Of course they do," Aunt Tilde said. "Men buy food that's easy to cook. Just heat and serve."

"And … women don't do that?" This conversation was boggling my mind.

"Not like this," Mildred said decisively.

"It was a lot of canned and boxed foods," Aunt Tilde said. "More like what a typical man would buy."

I wondered if I should ask how they had such intimate knowledge of the items Gin had purchased, but I decided I didn't want to know. "But you didn't take any pictures of Gin, right?"

Aunt Tilde turned to Nora. "Emily is right. We probably should have taken a photo."

"We need to remember for next time," Nora agreed.

"No, that's not what I'm saying," I said. "You shouldn't have taken any photos of Gin. She's not a client. I'm trying to get a handle on what you did take photos of. Like did you take any pictures of the husband or just owls and sunsets?"

"No, we got some pictures of him, as well," Aunt Tilde said, and I immediately let out a deep breath. *Thank goodness.* "We took those other shots to practice using the camera, is all."

"Plus, it helped pass the time," Nora said. "There's a lot of sitting around waiting at stakeouts."

"Yes, I've been told," I said. "But you did get photos of the husband?" I needed to be sure.

"Absolutely," Aunt Tilde said, bobbing her head. "We took pictures of him at his office, in his car, at his gym, at business meetings. All sorts of places."

"So, what's the problem then?" I asked, looking at Mildred, who still looked dejected.

"We failed," Mildred moaned, slumping in her seat.

"But you got photos of the husband," I said. "How did you fail?"

"We didn't get him with his mistress," Mildred said. "Not a single photo of his mistress."

"But maybe that's because he doesn't have a mistress," I said.

"Of course he has a mistress," Mildred said, exasperated. "We just weren't good enough to catch him with her."

"But I thought the whole point was to investigate whether or not he had a mistress," I said. "Not to assume he has one."

"I never assumed," Nora said. "And after getting to know him, I don't think he was cheating on his wife."

"You helped him up after your cat knocked him over," Mildred said. "That's hardly getting to know him."

"You can get to know someone by how they handle a setback," Nora said.

Mildred shook her head in disgust and gave her a sideways look. "Well, it doesn't matter now. Jan isn't going to pay if we don't give her results. And we didn't get results."

I wasn't sure that not finding proof of infidelity was the same as not getting results, but I had a feeling that wasn't going to sway Mildred. "You know, it's possible that Jan had it wrong," I said. "Just because she thought her husband was cheating on her doesn't mean he actually was."

"The wife always knows," Mildred said.

"Not necessarily. And besides, maybe there's something else going on altogether," I said.

Mildred threw me a suspicious look. "Like what?"

"Like maybe there's something going on with Jan," I said.

Nora scrunched up her eyebrows. "With Jan? What would be going on with her?"

"Well …" I felt like I had to tread carefully, as I remembered how the last conversation about Jan went. "Maybe she wasn't completely … honest with us?"

Nora looked more puzzled. "But she's our client."

"True …"

"Why would our client lie to us?"

"If she has ulterior motives," I said.

"But she's our client," Nora said again. "We're on her side, so that doesn't make any sense."

"I don't think she's lying to us," Mildred said, her voice firm. "And I'm an excellent judge of character."

It was all I could do to not roll my eyes.

"Emily might be on to something," Aunt Tilde said.

Nora stared at Aunt Tilde. "Now you think our client lied to us, too?"

"Maybe 'lied' is too strong a word," Aunt Tilde said. "Maybe she just didn't tell us the whole truth because she didn't think it was relevant to the case, but as it turns out, she was mistaken."

"I don't buy it," Mildred said. "All we're doing is making excuses for failing our client when we should be figuring out what we did wrong, so it won't happen again." She shot Nora a hard look.

Clearly, I wasn't getting anywhere, so I decided to switch tacks. "Well, you can always try again," I said. "Maybe wait a few days and do another stakeout."

Mildred shook her head before glowering at Nora. "No, we can't. Because her cat destroyed our cover, and now, he knows who we are. You think he won't be suspicious if he sees us hanging around again?"

Oh, I had forgotten about that. Mildred was right—that might get a little tricky.

"It's not Smoke's fault," Nora said, bending down to pet Smoke again. Smoke stopped cleaning himself long enough to sharply bat her hand away. She jerked her hand back and started to examine it. "You just never liked him. You always preferred Sherlock."

"Sherlock wasn't on a stakeout with us, so yes, in this instance, I absolutely do prefer Sherlock," Mildred said.

Sherlock began to purr, as if agreeing with her. Smoke looked up and started to meow loudly.

"See, look what you've done," Nora cried as she attempted to pet Smoke again, who still wasn't having any of it. "You've gotten everyone upset."

Mildred rolled her eyes as she muttered something under her breath.

"Emily, what did we miss?" Aunt Tilde asked. "Any calls or updates?"

"Well, actually, I do have an update for you, on the missing dog case," I said.

"You mean the one where Trisha dreamed that her aunt had a dog that went missing?" Mildred asked.

"Um …" I wasn't sure how to answer that. "Sort of. But that's not what happened."

Aunt Tilde's eyes lit up. "Oh, did you get her to admit she had a dog? Like Perry Mason?"

"Why would she admit to having a dog that Trisha dreamed about?" Mildred asked.

Nora's brows knitted together. "I thought that case was over. Didn't you find the dog?"

"No, this is the first dog. The one Gin says she never had," I said.

Nora looked even more perplexed. "If she didn't have a dog, then how could it be missing?"

"And that's the point," I said. "Trisha told us her aunt Gin had a dog that went missing a year ago. But when I asked Gin, she said she never had a dog. I told Trisha that was what her aunt said, and initially, Trisha was surprised and said she'd look into it. But then she told me that she had been mistaken, and Gin was right … she didn't have a dog after all."

"But that doesn't sense," Nora said. "Why would Trisha tell you her aunt had a dog if she didn't?"

"Because Trisha dreamed it all," Mildred repeated. "She did that a lot when she was a child. Always making things up."

"That may have been the case when she was a child, but I don't think she made this up," I said.

"Why not?" Aunt Tilde asked.

I took a deep breath. "Because her neighbor confirms Gin DID have a dog. A German shepherd named Rex. And that dog did go missing a year ago."

Silence. The other three looked at one another.

"I don't understand," Nora finally said. "Why would Gin lie about having a dog that went missing?"

"And why would Trisha back up that lie?" Aunt Tilde asked, eying Mildred. "Did Trisha ever do this as a child?"

Mildred looked flummoxed. "No, nothing like this. She was a flighty child, a bit of a dreamer, and would sometimes get confused as to what was real and what was in her head, but she never did anything maliciously. She would just get a little … mixed up. Not one of my brightest students, you understand, but she wasn't prone to lying or being mean to people."

"Maybe she was trying to protect her aunt," Aunt Tilde said.

"From what?" Mildred asked. "You think her aunt did something to the dog?"

"Is that so unbelievable?" Aunt Tilde asked.

"But she got another one," Nora said. "That doesn't sound like someone who would hurt a dog."

"Who said anything about it being on purpose?" Aunt Tilde said. "Maybe it was an accident, but she's embarrassed and doesn't want anyone to know."

"Or maybe she did do something illegal, and she's trying to cover it up," Mildred said, warming to the story. "Maybe there's something buried in the backyard Gin would rather no one know about."

"You mean like Gin killed someone and buried him in her backyard?" Aunt Tilde asked.

Mildred pointed at her. "That's exactly what I'm thinking."

"Wait, what?" On second thought, maybe I shouldn't have said anything.

"Except why would Gin kill someone?" Nora asked.

"Maybe someone killed the dog, and Gin killed him in revenge," Aunt Tilde said.

"Or, maybe the *dog* killed the person," Mildred said. "And Gin had no choice but to bury the body in the backyard."

"But where is the dog then?" Nora asked.

"Well, she'd have to hide the dog to protect him," Mildred said. "She can't let anyone know what happened."

"Oh, you're right. I bet that's what happened," Aunt Tilde said. "Gin was just trying to protect her dog."

"That's certainly one possibility," I said. "But there could be another explanation."

"That's true," Mildred said, tapping her bottom lip with her finger. "Which is why there's only one thing we can do."

"What's that?" Nora asked.

"Dig up her backyard, of course," Mildred said.

At that moment, the bell on the front door tinkled, and Nick walked in. "Whose backyard are you going to dig up?"

Mildred turned to him and narrowed her eyes. "How well do you know Trisha?"

Nick stared at her. "Um … is there a reason for that question?"

Mildred put her hands on her hips. "Why won't you just answer it? What are you hiding?"

Nick's eyes widened in surprise, but he quickly rearranged his features into a neutral expression. "I wasn't aware I was hiding anything."

Mildred gave him an exasperated look. "Are you kidding me? You're a lawyer. Of course you're hiding something. Probably lots of things." She straightened up and set a steely-eyed glare on him. "Do NOT try your lawyer tricks on me, young man. You forget who you're talking to."

"I absolutely have not forgotten who I'm talking to," Nick said meekly, although I could detect a gleam in his eyes. "Why don't we make a deal? You tell me why you want to know about Trisha, and I'll tell you what I know."

"Does she have a backyard?" Nora asked.

Nick whipped his head around to her. "What? You want to dig up Trisha's backyard?"

"Of course not," Aunt Tilde said. "Nora is just being thorough."

Nick's eyes went wide. "Thorough?"

"Well, you never know," Nora said. "It could run in the family."

Nick's eyes narrowed. "*What* could run in the family?"

"Nick, why are you here?" I quickly jumped in before the situation derailed even more than it already had. I was instantly terrified of Mildred sneaking into Gin's backyard in the dead of night, shovel in hand, with Nora and Aunt Tilde bringing up the rear, and probably Smoke trailing along after them. The only thing that could be worse was if she added Trisha's backyard to her to-do list. "Is there something you need?"

"I just thought I'd knock off early this afternoon, as it's Friday, and do some work on the kitchen," Nick said, but he wasn't looking at me. He was still warily watching the other three women.

"Oh, that's so nice of you," I said nervously. "We appreciate that."

"We definitely do," Aunt Tilde said, moving toward the coffeepot. "Would you like a cup of coffee or a soda before you get started? I was just going to make a fresh pot."

Nick hadn't moved. He was still giving Mildred and Nora the side-eye. "What I'd like is to know more about why you're suddenly so interested in backyards."

"For garden ideas," I said quickly as I watched Mildred open her mouth to respond. "Mildred was thinking about redoing her backyard. Right?"

Mildred closed her mouth and shot me an indecipherable look. "Yes. I've been thinking about adding more … flowers."

Nick gave her a hard look. I could tell he wasn't convinced, but he didn't push it. "Okay then. I guess I'll go get started. And to answer your question, no, Trisha doesn't have a garden. She lives in a condo."

"Guess we can cross her off the list," Mildred said.

"What list?" Nick barked out.

"The list of people with gardens Mildred can check out," I said swiftly, glaring at Mildred. Mildred clamped her mouth shut.

Nick gave us all a long, suspicious look before heading into the kitchen.

"Emily, you should have let me interrogate him," Mildred hissed. "How are we going to find the body if we can't ask questions?"

"We don't know if there even is a body," I said, equally hushed. "There might be other reasons why Gin is lying about having another dog."

"Oh, like what?" Mildred demanded, folding her arms across her chest.

I shuffled through the stack of paper on my desk, uncovering the photocopy I had made of the newspaper article. "A year ago, a dog walker named Ed Wheeler went missing."

"Oh, I remember that," Nora said. "He trained dogs, too, didn't he? One of my customers used to take lessons from him. She was really worried about him. Do they know what happened to him?"

"No, unfortunately not," I said.

"So, what are you saying? You think Gin killed this dog trainer and buried him in her backyard?" Mildred asked.

"Wait, what? No, that's not what I'm saying at all," I said.

"Maybe he helped Gin bury the body," Nora said.

"Forget the dead body," I said. "What I'm saying is maybe Ed is the one who took Gin's dog."

The three women stared blankly at me. "You think Gin's dog was dognapped?" Aunt Tilde asked.

"Yeah, I think that's a possibly. Don't you?"

"But why would this dog walker steal a dog?" Nora asked.

"And why would Gin lie about having a dog, if hers was taken?" Aunt Tilde said.

"I don't know," I said, feeling myself start to deflate. Ugh, there really were a lot more questions than answers.

"And do you know if they even knew each other?" Aunt Tilde asked. "Did the neighbor ever see him walk Gin's dog?"

"Okay, look, I don't have the answers. Yet," I said, putting the article on my desk and pointing at it. "But look at the timing. It was about a year ago when Ed went missing, which is the same time Gin's dog went missing."

Aunt Tilde came over to peer at the newspaper article. "But we still don't know if they knew each other."

"The neighbor said Gin had taken the dog to a trainer," I said.

Aunt Tilde's eyes went wide. "Oh, so she was going to the trainer who disappeared."

"Well, the neighbor didn't actually know who the trainer was," I said reluctantly.

Aunt Tilde stared at me. "So it might not have been Ed."

"But it might have been," I said, even as I was thinking to myself that I was sounding more and more like Mildred. "We don't know either way. But don't you think it's worth investigating?"

"Of course it is," Aunt Tilde said. "Especially as we now know Gin was lying about the dog, so she's definitely hiding something. We just need to figure out what."

"Absolutely! We need to get to the bottom of this," Mildred said before shooting me an almost sympathetic gaze. "But I wouldn't hold my breath with this dog-walker angle. Seems a little far-fetched to me."

I let out a strangled gasp that sounded more like I was choking. Far-fetched? Says the woman who wanted to dig up Gin's backyard to look for a corpse?

But before I could come up with a suitable response, the tinkling of the bell on the front door interrupted me.

Chapter 15

"Hey, is Nick here? Oh …"

Trisha breezed in, the scent of her perfume and spearmint gum wafting past us. She paused uncertainly and stared. "Sorry, am I interrupting something?"

"Actually, your timing is perfect," Mildred said, ignoring my pointed stare.

Trisha looked even more uncertain. "Oh?"

"Yes," Mildred said, standing up and walking around her desk to step closer to Trisha as she continued to ignore me and my now frantic hand gestures indicating for her to stop. "There was a development in your aunt's case, and we wanted to ask you …"

Trisha interrupted her. "My aunt's case? What case?" The shrillness in her tone was something I hadn't heard before.

Mildred seemed unperturbed. "The one about your aunt's dog that went missing a year ago …"

"There is no case," she snapped. "There can't be, because there's no dog." She whirled around toward me. "I told you I was mistaken, and there was no dog."

"I know you did," I said, keeping my voice level. The wildness in her eyes was causing alarm bells to sound off in my head. "But Trisha, it doesn't make sense … that you would make that sort of mistake."

"How do you know what I would or would not do?" Trisha practically shouted at me. "I made a mistake, okay? I'm human. Humans make mistakes."

"Okay," I said again, both palms out, trying desperately to pacify her. Never in my wildest dreams had I expected this reaction. I figured she might get upset, but I never anticipated a freakout. And based on the wide-eyed stares of Nora and Aunt Tilde, they hadn't expected it either. Even Mildred looked taken aback. "I'm not trying to upset you."

"Then why don't you just drop it?" Trisha snapped.

"Okay, but the thing is, your aunt's neighbor …"

"What's going on out here?" Nick came tearing out of the kitchen, skidding to a stop when he saw Trisha. "Trisha? What are you doing here?"

Trisha turned on him. "I told you I made a mistake! Why are you going on and on about this?"

"Um, okay," Nick said, trying to look at all of us at once. He ran his hand through his hair. "Trish, I'm not sure what you're referring to?"

She folded her arms across her chest. "The dog. Aunt Gin's dog. I told you I made a mistake. Why can't all of you just drop it?"

He looked genuinely baffled. "Trisha, I have no idea what you're talking about."

She gave him a withering glance. "They're still hanging around my aunt's house asking questions that are none of their business!"

"I …" Nick gave me a sideways glance. "You're going to have to fill me in, as I'm really not sure what's going on."

"Oh, forget it!" Trisha threw up her hands. "Just forget it." She turned on her heel and stormed out of the agency, leaving the rest of us staring after her in utter befuddlement.

"Um." Nick's eyes darted between us and the door that had slammed shut behind her. "I think … maybe I should go check on her."

"Yes, you should," Aunt Tilde said at the same time Mildred said, "Well, someone should."

Nick gave us an uneasy look before hurrying out the door. My stomach clenched as I watched him go, knowing he was choosing her (never mind that she was his girlfriend, and he ought to).

Still, it left me feeling hollow inside.

Mildred shook her head sadly. "That's a guilty conscience if I ever saw one."

"I bet she helped dig the hole," Nora said.

"Or maybe she was the one who accidentally killed someone," Mildred said. "And Gin was trying to protect her."

"I don't think Trisha had anything to do with what happened to Gin's dog," I said, although I wasn't sure if I was trying to convince myself or them. Trisha's reaction had left me feeling a little shaken. Under the desk, I felt a cool nose press against my hand, and I buried my hands in Scout's soft, warm fur, already feeling more grounded.

Mildred frowned at me. "Are you kidding me? Of course she did. Why else would she react like that?"

"I have no idea what's going on with her, but why would she tell us to investigate her aunt's dog in the first place, if she knew there was a dead body buried in her aunt's backyard?"

Mildred opened her mouth, closed it, and tapped her lips with her finger.

"That's a good point," Nora said.

"Yes, but there's definitely *something* going on," Mildred said. "Maybe her aunt confessed the whole sordid mess to her, and she doesn't want to see her aunt go to jail."

"Oh man … can you imagine how guilty she would feel if that happened?" Nora said. "Knowing she was the one who initiated an investigation by involving you. Although the good news is that we would at least know what happened to the dog walker."

"I …" I started to respond but promptly gave up. As much as I didn't think the dog walker was buried in Gin's backyard, I had to admit there was something very fishy with Trisha's reaction.

But how would I find out the truth?

***

I was still puzzling over Trisha's odd outburst and how to uncover the truth when Jerome suddenly snapped his fingers in front of me. "Earth to Emily. Again."

I flushed, embarrassed that this was the second time Jerome had caught me not paying attention, before busying myself with my crystal water glass, hoping the ice water would cool my heated cheeks. "Oh, sorry."

We were at an upscale steak and seafood restaurant called The Terrace, which was near the outskirts of town. It was all white and black: white tablecloths, white cloth napkins, and tall white candles providing a warm glow against black chairs and the clothing of the waitstaff. It was much nicer, and much pricier, than anything I would expect for a second official date, and there I was mulling about a missing dog rather than focusing on him. Ugh.

Jerome tilted his head as he reached for his beer. "Is there anything wrong? You're pretty preoccupied."

"Yeah, sorry, it's just this case." I reached for a breadstick and broke off a piece.

He furrowed his brow. "The … missing dog case?"

I nodded and reached for the butter. I had already filled him in earlier, both today and on previous dates. "Now that I know for sure that Gin and Trisha were both lying about Gin owning a dog, I have to figure out what to do next."

He gave me a funny look. "Why?"

"Because I don't know how to uncover the truth when both of them are lying. Who else can I ask who might know why they would lie about such a thing?"

"No, I mean, why are you still worried about this case?"

Now it was my turn to give him a funny look. "Isn't it obvious? Because they're lying to everyone, and it makes no sense. Why lie about something as insignificant as a missing dog?"

He pointed at me. "Exactly my point. Why do you care so much about something as insignificant as a missing dog?"

My eyes widened. "But … that's not insignificant."

"You just said it was."

"Yes, but that's not what I meant." My voice rose higher. "It's not against the law for a dog to go missing. So why lie about it? Why not just say, 'Yes my dog went missing a year ago, but I don't think there's anything you can do'? No one would have blinked an eye at that. Instead, Tricia made up a lie about there being no dog when there was one. Why would anyone do that? In this case, the cover-up seems worse than the crime."

He gave me an exasperated look. "Emily, it's a missing dog. How bad can the crime be?"

"Well, according to Mildred, there might be a body buried in Gin's backyard. So yeah, it could be bad."

He rolled his eyes. "You and I both know Mildred likes to exaggerate. I'm sure there's nothing of the sort going on. Whatever it is, it's probably just embarrassing to this aunt, and she wants everyone to drop it."

"But that's my point. If she hadn't lied about it, everyone would have dropped it. So why lie?"

He spread his hands out in front of him. "Why does anyone do anything? People do stupid things all the time. It doesn't mean anything, and it certainly doesn't mean there's anything nefarious going on under the surface."

"Yes, but in this case, there's so many things that don't add up. Why ask us to look into it in the first place? Why lie about not having a dog? Why tell me that you made a mistake about your aunt owning a dog? And then, to top it off, get so upset when you're questioned about it? Something strange is going on."

"Maybe. Or maybe it's just weird family dynamics that are none of your business."

I jerked my head back like he slapped me. "None of my business? But I was asked to look into it."

"That's true, but it doesn't look like the family wants you to look into it anymore, does it?"

"But …" I wasn't sure what to say to that. I also couldn't believe I was having this argument with Jerome. "But don't you want to know why?"

He shrugged and picked up his beer. "Not particularly, no. And I don't know why you're so interested in it either. It's a missing dog. It's sad, but dogs go missing all the time." He turned his head as our waitress started toward us, carrying our meals on a tray. "Oh, here's our food. Perfect timing. Let's take a breath and enjoy our dinner. Would you like another glass of wine?"

I looked down at my plate of grilled salmon on a bed of wild rice and tried to sort out what I was feeling. Was Jerome right, and I was interfering in things that were none of my business?

Or was there really something suspicious going on that I needed to get to the bottom of?

Chapter 16

I was still stewing about my date with Jerome as I weeded Aunt Tilde's garden the next day. Scout had joined me, alternating between lounging in the shade and nosing me for petting, the latter being instigated when he seemed to sense my thoughts veering off in an agitated direction. Then, I would stroke his warm fur, smelling of sun and cut grass, and feel myself relax. He was turning out to be more calming than Charlie Kingsley's lemon-lavender tea.

The rest of the evening with Jerome had gone … okay, I guess. He had made a point of asking me a lot of questions, but of course, nothing about the agency or cases, and I just couldn't shake my irritation. How could he not be even the slightest bit curious as to why Trisha and Gin lied? That just seemed completely unnatural.

But then, I would remember him telling me how it was none of my business, and I would find myself going hot then cold then hot again.

Was I meddling in things I shouldn't be? Had I become the nosy, interfering busybody no one liked?

I never used to worry about the type of person I was. I never used to worry that I had crossed a line and was sticking my nose into things I had no business "investigating." Of course, at that time, I was living a lie and was completely oblivious to it.

Maybe I would have been better off if someone—anyone—had decided to not mind their own business and instead asked me all sorts of impertinent and nosy questions. Maybe I would have seen through the illusion before it all came crashing down around me.

Scout suddenly let out a friendly woof, startling me out of my thoughts. He bounded away, yellow tail wagging. I turned to see Nick standing at the end of the yard, Scout happily greeting him.

I stood up, feeling self-conscious in my worn, faded, frayed jean shorts and skin-tight, yellow tank top with dirt smudged across it.

Even worse, I had topped the outfit off with a pink floppy hat I borrowed from Aunt Tilde. I hadn't taken a shower that day, simply pulled my hair back into a messy ponytail under the hat and gone out to attack the weeds in the yard, and now I was wishing I had done … something different.

It was too late to worry about any of that, though, as Nick had finished petting Scout and was heading toward me. "Hey, I hope it's okay I stopped by. I don't know your number, or I would have called first."

I wiped the sweat from my forehead and immediately regretted it. With my luck, I'd just smeared dirt across my forehead, too. "It's fine. I've been out here most of the day anyhow, so I probably wouldn't have heard the phone ring."

He stopped and put his hands in his pockets, shifting his weight back and forth. He wore jeans and a green tee shirt that brought out the green in his eyes and the broadness of his chest. "I don't want to bother you. I can come back another time if you'd like."

"No, it's fine. I could use a break anyway. Want to sit for a moment, maybe have some water or lemonade?" I nodded toward the porch, where a glass table and black wrought-iron chairs sat.

"Sure, if it's not too much trouble," he said.

"No trouble. Just give me a minute." I waved him toward the chairs and hurried into Aunt Tilde's house. I already knew she was out for the afternoon, although I wasn't entirely sure what she was doing. She had mentioned something about volunteering and a bridge tournament, although I wasn't clear if that was two different things, or related. I also knew she had a pitcher of homemade lemonade in the fridge, so I quickly fetched it and two glasses. I really wanted to duck into the bathroom and do something about my appearance, but I thought that might be too obvious, so I gritted my teeth and went back outside.

Scout had his head in Nick's lap, his tongue lolling as Nick massaged his ears. I filled the two glasses and pushed one in front of him as I sat down in the opposite chair.

"Thanks," he said, taking a long drink. "I always liked Tilde's lemonade. Not too tart, not too sweet."

"Agreed."

Scout nudged Nick's hand, and Nick reached over and continued rubbing his ears. "I feel like I owe you an apology," he said finally.

I looked at him in surprise. "What for?"

He grimaced. "Trisha."

"Why do you need to apologize for Trisha? She's a grown woman."

He picked up his glass, draining half of it, then set it back down on the table. "I should have warned you not to bring anything up if you happened to see her. That was my plan, actually ... to warn you. But I was waiting to catch you alone. I thought there might be fewer questions that way."

"Yeah, I can see that," I said, thinking about Mildred's reaction to Nick telling her not to talk to Trisha. She would probably try to make a citizen's arrest on Trisha, sure she was guilty of something.

"Anyway, I didn't think Trisha would show up at the agency, or I would have said something sooner. Especially since I had a feeling that's what you were talking about when I walked in." He threw me a knowing look. "Do I even want to know why Mildred is suddenly so interested in backyards?"

"Not particularly," I said. "But what is the deal with Trisha? Do you know why she got so upset?"

He was silent for a long moment, staring at his lemonade glass as if watching the condensation slowly drip down the side was the key to finding the meaning of life. "I'm going to tell you something, but please don't share it with anyone else."

A frisson of electricity ran down my spine, and I leaned forward slightly. "Of course."

He eyed me. "I'm serious. Not even Tilde."

"My lips are sealed." I mimed locking my mouth and throwing away the key.

His own lips quirked up slightly. "Okay. So I wasn't actually honest with you at the coffee shop."

Of all the things I thought he might say, I wasn't expecting that. "What do you mean?"

"When you asked about Trisha not remembering that her aunt had a dog or not, or ..." he rolled his eyes, "maybe dreaming about the dog. There is actually some history there. I just never imagined that this dog business would have anything to do with it."

I cocked my head. "You mean, Trisha does have memory issues?"

"No, she doesn't. Not really. But she's really sensitive about it, and …" He looked up at the sky for a moment and ran a hand through his hair. "I guess I should just start at the beginning. When Trisha was a child, like six or seven, somewhere in there, she was in a pretty bad car accident that left her with a severe concussion."

My eyes widened. "Seriously?"

"Yeah. It was so bad, the doctors thought she might have permanent brain damage. For a long time, she had problems with her memory, but eventually, her brain healed, and she was fine. Anyway, because of this, she can be … sensitive, when she forgets something or has trouble understanding something."

I held up a hand. "Wait a minute. Are you saying that Mildred was actually right, and Trisha DID have memory issues or problems telling the difference between dreams and reality?"

Nick nodded. "I know. It's kind of nuts, but yes. Mildred was absolutely right. Again, it was a long time ago, and Trisha is fine. Yes, she occasionally forgets things, but who doesn't? I never thought for a moment there was anything wrong with her. But again, she's sensitive about it. She doesn't like to talk about it. I think she might have been teased or bullied when she was still recovering.

"Anyway, when you told me that she's now changing her story about Gin having a dog, I honestly thought she was most likely trying to protect Gin. From what, I couldn't fathom. It never occurred to me that Trisha truly had changed her story and was now claiming she had gotten it wrong. So, when I asked her about it, I was not prepared for how upset she got, or how she kept insisting this was her fault. She also wanted me to be more understanding, knowing her history. I told her there was nothing wrong with her brain, and that I specifically remember her talking about her aunt's dog going missing. That only upset her more, and she began claiming it was actually her cousin's dog that had gone missing …"

"Wait a minute," I interrupted a second time. "She actually said that? That her *cousin's* dog had gone missing?"

"Yeah, why? Is that important?"

"No, not really. It's just … go on." First, Mildred was right about Trisha having issues when she was a child, and now, Trisha was using Mildred's cousin excuse? If Mildred found out, I might never hear the end of it.

"Well, there isn't much to say. The conversation went downhill from there. She kept insisting it wasn't her fault—that her brain didn't always work right. She wanted to know why I was making such a big thing of it in the first place. It was just a missing dog, after all. Not like a person going missing."

I started, like I had been poked in the back with something sharp. Maybe an icicle, because shivers shot down my spine. "She said that? A missing person?"

"Yes." Nick's eyes narrowed. "Why? What do you know about a missing person?"

"It's probably not related," I said slowly.

Nick leaned forward slightly. "What isn't related?"

I sighed. "It's just … I found this article in *The Riverview Times.*"

"When? Today?"

"No, a year ago."

His eyebrows went up. "Ah, so that's what's going on. You were researching this, weren't you?"

I held my hands up. "Guilty as charged. I just couldn't let it go, so I went to the library to look at back copies of the paper. And I discovered that a man named Ed Wheeler went missing about this time last year."

Nick frowned. "Name doesn't ring a bell, but that doesn't mean anything. A lot of people go missing in this town."

"So I've noticed. Anyway, Ed had a little side business helping people with their dogs. Dog walker, dog trainer, maybe other things."

Nick's body tensed. "Did he and Gin know each other? Like, did Gin use him for dog walking or training?"

I shook my head. "I actually don't know. But what I know for sure is that Gin was lying. As, it would seem, was Trisha."

He straightened at my last sentence. "Oh?"

"The neighbor. She told me that yes, Gin had a dog before Rocky, and that dog did indeed disappear. His name was Rex, and he was a German shepherd."

I paused, waiting for Nick to say something, but he stayed silent as he simply stared at me. There was a strange expression in his eyes, one I couldn't read, so I kept talking. "Rocky, that's her dog now, is one of those little white fluffy dogs. Blythe, that's her neighbor, isn't a fan of little dogs—she prefers the German shepherd, but of course, it's not her choice, so-"

"Are you sure?" Nick interrupted. His green eyes had sharpened, and I started to feel uncomfortable … like I was now the one being cross-examined.

"Well, as sure as I can be without actually seeing the dog for myself," I said. "Blythe was pretty convincing."

"Does she know what happened to … what was his name? Was it Rex?"

"Yes, that was his name, and no, she doesn't. She was at a doctor's appointment all day, and when she got home, he was gone."

"Did Gin tell her what happened to Rex?"

"Gin told Blythe that Rex had gotten out of the yard, but …" I chewed on my bottom lip, wondering how far down the rabbit hole I should go. "Blythe didn't believe it."

"Really?" Nick considered this. "What does she think happened?"

"Most likely that Rex got hit by a car and was killed. Gin never wanted to talk about Rex again, so Blythe thought Gin blamed herself for Rex's death."

Nick nodded absently, his gaze far away. Scout nudged him again, and he commenced rubbing his ears yet again. "That makes sense, in a way, although it doesn't explain why Trisha decided to change her story and pretend she was having some sort of injury-related brain fart. Did Blythe have any other theories?"

"Um …" Nick had caught me off guard. I hadn't intended on mentioning the Rex-was-kidnapped-by-crazed-stalkers theory.

His gaze hardened into his lawyer look. "What is it?"

"It's really … kind of stupid, actually. Not to mention complicated."

His eyes bored into me. "Tell me anyway." His voice was light, belying the intensity of his gaze.

I swallowed. "It's so complicated, I can't remember it all, but in a nutshell, she thinks Rex might have been … dognapped. And that

Gin is too frightened to say anything, lest the dognappers come back."

I expected him to laugh, but if anything, he seemed even more grave. "Actually, that idea makes more sense, in terms of Trisha's reaction."

I could feel my jaw drop. He was taking this seriously?

"I'm sorry?"

"If she was worried about her aunt's safety, then yeah. Think about it. If her aunt's life could actually be in danger, the last thing she would want is someone digging into this."

"But …" I was so floored, I actually couldn't find any words. "Why would anyone steal a dog? It makes no sense."

Nick sat back, his brow furrowed. "I know. It doesn't. But when you consider that this dog walker disappeared, and both of these women are lying outrageously about a missing dog, it does make you wonder what's really going on."

I was too dumbfounded to answer. The idea that a sweet German shepherd (well, sweet according to Blythe) had been kidnapped seemed preposterous.

Yet here was Nick, taking it seriously.

Maybe there really was something deeper and darker going on than simply a missing dog.

Chapter 17

I parked on the side of the street next to the dog park, but didn't turn the car off. Instead, I just sat there for a moment, letting the car idle as Scout hung his head out the back window.

Nick was the one who told me about this dog park. "Have you checked it out? It's pretty nice," he said as he rubbed Scout's ears. "If you find a map of Redemption, I can show you where it is." It was such a non sequitur from our earlier conversation that I wasn't even sure how to respond, so I fetched a map so he could show me. It wasn't until I took a closer look that I saw it was only a few blocks from Gin's house. I shot him a quick glance, and he merely winked at me before draining his glass and telling me he had to go.

And even though I knew I really ought to be spending my time thinking about Gin and figuring out a way to approach her again, I instead found myself going back over my conversation with Nick, obsessively turning over each detail.

Which made no sense. We weren't together. We were barely friends, if you could even call whatever our relationship was "friends." I wasn't sure what to call it.

But none of that mattered, because he was with Trisha, and I was with Jerome. Sort of. Maybe. Or maybe not, since I was still irked about our last date. I had played it cool when he asked me about seeing me again, saying I needed to check my calendar. I also hadn't returned his call. The more I thought about it, the more the whole thing bothered me. I couldn't put my finger on it until I realized it was like being with Geoff all over again. Being dismissive of subjects that were important to me and not taking me seriously. Maybe this whole thing was a mistake. He had me feel so … small.

Just like Geoff used to.

But never mind Jerome. Once this was over, I could figure out what I wanted to do about him. In the current moment, my concern was Nick, even if a part of me knew it really shouldn't be.

I mean, so what that he stopped by to apologize for Trisha? It didn't mean anything. Just like it didn't mean anything that we sat outside discussing the case. Or the strange, intense way he looked at me as he was about to leave—almost like he wanted to tell me something but then changed his mind at the last minute and turned away.

None of that mattered. He was with Trisha. Period. And regardless of what happened with Jerome, I needed to get that through my head.

I sucked in a deep breath, forcing myself to stop thinking about Nick—about how his green eyes turned dark when he was thinking deeply, or the way his lips would twitch into a half-smile when he was amused by something—to start focusing on the reason why I was sitting in my car in front of a dog park, squinting at the handful of people and dogs in the fenced area to see if Gin was there.

Of course, she wasn't. And even though Scout was eagerly staring at the dog park, his tail thumping madly, I was hesitant to take him over. What if Gin showed up and saw me there? It might frighten her away, and then what was I going to do?

As I sat in the car mulling my options, Scout kept his head out the window, tongue lolling in the sun. A compact blue car puttered up and turned into the parking lot. As I watched, Gin got out, barely hanging onto an extremely excited Rocky, whose tail was wagging so frantically, I was sure she was going to drop him. She awkwardly carried him to the gate, where they were met by what I assumed to be the Welcoming Committee, which consisted of a chocolate lab, a golden retriever, and a standard poodle. It was a bit of a tussle getting through the gate, but eventually, Gin got it sorted out, and Rocky and the Welcoming Committee were joyously greeting one another other like they hadn't played together in years. Gin waved at a couple of older women sitting at a picnic table under a pavilion. They waved back, one of them busy fanning herself, and Gin headed toward them.

I couldn't believe my luck. Quickly, I got out of the car and let Scout out, and after attaching the leash to his collar, we hurried over to the dog park.

It was easier for me to get in, as the Welcoming Committee was still busy with Rocky, but they quickly realized they were derelict in their duties and rushed back to greet both Scout and me. Once we were all friends and they ran off to play, I started walking toward Gin, who had yet to notice me as she was busy chatting.

Scout suddenly broke off from the other dogs, lopping past me and right up to Gin. Gin laughed as Scout thrust his head onto her lap, and she started stroking his ears.

I couldn't believe it. It was perfect. I hadn't quite worked out how I was going to approach her, short of just going up to her, but Scout just gave me the perfect opening. I sped up my pace. "Sorry," I called out when I was closer. "But don't worry, he's friendly."

"I see that," Gin said with a smile, playfully pushing him away as she turned to me.

Her smile died on her face.

"Hi Gin," I said cheerfully as the other two women regarded me curiously. "It's nice to see you again."

She paused, swallowing hard, eying the other two women before looking at me. "Yes. I haven't seen you here before."

"Oh, well, I didn't know about this dog park until today. I'm still relatively new to Redemption," I said breezily.

"Oh, where are you from?" the woman fanning herself asked me. She wore a white, wide-brimmed hat, a pale-pink top covered in embroidered flowers, and a pair of white pants.

"Riverview," I said.

Her eyes widened. "Oh, this must be a different experience for you then."

"Yes, it definitely is, but I'm enjoying it."

Gin stood up abruptly. "Oh, look at Rocky. I probably should check on him and make sure he's not bothering the other dogs. Want to come with, and I can introduce you to all the pups?" She turned toward me, giving me a hard look, and I tried to remember if I introduced myself or not when I went to her house.

"Sure, that would be great," I said as she led me away from the pavilion and toward Rocky, who was playing with the chocolate lab. Scout ran ahead of us and joined them. Two other women were sitting on a park bench on the other side of the dog park. They waved at Gin, who waved back at them.

"What do you want?" Her voice was low, and she kept her head down. I considered telling her I was there for Scout, but decided not to play games.

"I just have a couple more questions for you."

"I told you, I didn't have a dog that went missing." She sounded like she was gritting her teeth, but she kept her voice quiet.

"Your neighbor Blythe remembers things differently," I said.

She stopped dead, her head snapping up. "You're investigating me? After I told you not to?"

I stopped as well, turning to face her. "You didn't tell me not to investigate you. You told me you didn't have a dog that went missing. And then Trisha suddenly tells me she made a mistake, and there was no dog. You can't tell me you wouldn't find that strange, if you were me."

"What. Do. You. Want." She practically spat each word out of her mouth, like the words were rotten.

I met her gaze. "The truth."

Her eyes went wide. "Why? Why do you care so much? You don't even know us."

"Maybe not. But do you truly think all this hiding is good for anyone? Trisha is a basket case, and Blythe is worried about you. Do you really think keeping secrets is healthy for anyone?"

"I don't ..." she stopped talking and ground her teeth together. "It's not my secret to tell."

For a moment, I almost couldn't believe it. Could I finally be getting somewhere? "Is it Ed Wheeler's?"

Her face went chalk white. "Who told you that name?" Her voice was a hiss.

"I read about his disappearance in the newspaper, and the timing seemed a little ... coincidental."

She closed her eyes tightly. "This is ... awful. How did this happen? He's going to be so upset with me."

I did a double take. He's going to be so upset with her? Did that mean … "Why don't you tell me about it? I'm not going to tell anyone, but I think it would be good for you if you finally told someone the truth."

She had started rubbing her temples, but paused and opened her eyes to study me. "At this point, I guess it doesn't matter, because you're probably going to keep poking around and doing more damage if I don't." She let out a loud sigh and dropped her hands. "Let's sit over there."

She led me to one of the park benches that was about as far away from everyone else as it could get. Both Rocky and Scout happily followed us, along with the chocolate lab. She sat down heavily on one side, and Rocky jumped on her lap. I sat down next to her, but didn't say anything, letting her decide how she wanted to proceed.

"Since you talked to Blythe, you probably already know my husband died a few years ago. It hit me hard. For a long time, I couldn't leave the house. I was drowning in grief and wanted to die as well.

"It was Trisha who got me out of it. She told me Dan wouldn't have wanted to see me like that … that he would want me to live my life, not hide behind a curtain." She smiled at the memory. "That was something Dan said a lot. He would never spend his retirement years hiding behind a curtain. He'd be out living his life. So, I started forcing myself to go for walks, just to get out of the house. To my surprise, I discovered I liked walking. I was never much into exercising, so that was unexpected. Anyway, I decided to try hiking, and I found I liked that even more than walking around the neighborhood. So, I started doing longer hikes, and more often."

She paused and looked away. I could see she was fighting to compose her expression. "Everything was going so well. I had restarted my volunteering, and I was back to knitting and cooking, which were two things I loved to do, but had abandoned. I was able to start doing the normal, everyday stuff again, too, like taking regular showers and cleaning the house. When I was deep in the throes of grief, I couldn't even bring myself to do a load of laundry, so this was major progress. Even though I still missed Dan like crazy, the pain wasn't an intense as before. More of a dull ache. I felt like I was finally back in the land of the living. Until the day I met Ed."

She paused again, her fists tightening until the skin turned white. Her entire body had stiffened, and I could see her forcing herself to take deep breaths. "It was a day like any other. I had my volunteering in the morning, so I decided to take an afternoon hike. It was beautiful—the sun was out, but there was a nice, cool breeze, so it wasn't too hot. It was just perfect ... at least until those two perverts showed up."

My eyebrows went up. "Perverts? Do you mean ..."

She shuddered and shook her head violently. "Nothing happened to me. At least not physically. They just ..." she shivered again. "It was horrible. I was all alone on the path, and I knew they could easily overpower me, so I tried to get away, but they followed me. And the things they were saying ..." She pressed her hands over her ears for a moment and sucked in another deep breath. "I don't know what would have happened if Ed hadn't been there, but suddenly, just like that, he was there on the path with us.

"He knew immediately that there was a problem, and he confronted the two perverts. At first, they told him to get lost, but he simply instructed me to walk away instead. I was a little reluctant to leave him, as he was quite a bit older than the two perverts. But he was also very fit, and when he offered me a little smile and told me it would be fine, I did what I was told. After all, it wasn't like I would be of any help in a fight, so I figured the best thing I could do was get out of there as quickly as possible and call the police for help.

"It probably took about ten, fifteen minutes, but he did catch up to me. I asked him what happened, and he told me not to worry about it ... but that those two perverts wouldn't be bothering me anymore."

"Do you know what he did to them?"

She shook her head. "He never told me, and I never asked for specifics. It seemed better that way. Anyway, we got to talking, and eventually, he asked me if I had a dog. I told him I had never had a dog, and he said I might want to think about getting one—particularly, a big one, like a German shepherd or Rottweiler — to hike with me for protection. He said it would be a good deterrent to punks like those guys. I told him I didn't like big dogs, so if I ever got one, it would be little, like a Maltese or a Bichon Frise." She smiled faintly. "He said a dog like that wouldn't do much for protection, and besides, they weren't 'real' dogs anyway. He was joking about the last part, but not the first. I told him I'd consider it, but that wasn't true. I had no intention of getting a dog, big or otherwise. I figured once the shock of what happened wore off and I got a good night's sleep, I'd be fine, and everything would go back to the way it was.

"But that isn't what happened. I couldn't get past it. Every time I closed my eyes, I would see their taunting faces as they laughed at me. My ears burned with their ugly words." She shivered. "I could even *smell* them. They stunk of bad breath and sweat and terrible body order. It was horrible. I couldn't leave the house, not even to go to the grocery store, because I was terrified they would pop up, like a demented Jack-in-the-box. Except this time, there would be no Ed to save me.

"And before I knew it, I was right back where I had been a few months before. Cowering in my home. Afraid of my own shadow. The only difference was that this time, I was showering, albeit four or five times a day, so at least I was clean, even if I didn't feel like it.

"After a few weeks of this, I decided I wouldn't, I couldn't, do this to myself any longer. So I dug up Ed's phone number, which he had given me that day, telling me if I ever did get a dog, I should reach out, as he was a dog trainer. I called, and he asked me if I had gotten the dog yet. When I said no, he said he had the perfect dog for me. And that's how I got Rex."

"So did Ed know Rex's owner or something?"

She looked at me like I was a complete idiot. "Rex was Ed's dog."

"Ohhh." The pieces were starting to fall into place. "Ed gave you his dog?"

"He hadn't had him very long. Only about a month or so, but Rex was so smart, he had already learned the basics, like sitting for his food and being completely potty-trained. At first, I wasn't going to take him. Rex was his dog, after all, but Ed kept insisting it was fine. He wasn't in a great place to have his own dog anyway, and if I hired him for dog training, he could still see him. He was joking about the second part, but I jumped on that and said I would absolutely hire him. I also let him know that he was welcome to visit Rex any time."

She paused and chewed on her bottom lip. "I want you to understand, I didn't feel good about taking his dog. Not even a little bit. And if I hadn't been so desperate … if I couldn't feel the walls of my house closing in on me … if I wasn't having nightmares every night around that horrible day … I wouldn't have taken Rex. But I was desperate, so I did."

"You don't have to explain yourself to me," I said. "I get it. I probably would have done the same if I were in your shoes."

She looked at me then, for the first time since we had sat down on the bench. I could see the sadness in her eyes, but there was something else, as well. I couldn't explain it, but it seemed like gratitude. Maybe it was because someone was not only listening to her story, but understanding and sympathizing with her, as well.

"I second-guessed myself a lot," she said. "I told myself I should have been stronger … that I shouldn't have allowed myself to fall apart the way I did. But from the moment I brought Rex home, even though he was still a puppy, I felt better. Safer. Even though it made absolutely no sense, seeing as how Rex was too small to protect himself, much less me. But it didn't matter. I was no longer all alone in that house. There was another living creature with me, and more than that, he needed regular walks and training. And suddenly, I was back to my normal self. I had a schedule, a reason to get up and go outside every day. More than that, I had a friend."

She turned away and busied herself with her purse. She pulled out a tissue, and I could see the faint gleam of tears in her eyes, but she simply dabbed at them. I waited a few moments before finally asking, "What changed?"

She let out a bark of laughter that had no humor to it as she looked down at the tissue she was still clutching. "Justice, if you can believe it."

"What do you mean?"

She twisted the tissue into a tight ball. "Those perverts? They were finally caught by the police. One was a Peeping Tom, and the other did something equally disgusting."

My mind went back to the newspaper articles. Was it really possible those were the same two men who had harassed Gin? "I think I read something about them in the newspaper."

She sniffed. "Of course you did. Everyone did. Good riddance, I say. Except …" she let out a sigh. "This is the part of the story that isn't mine to tell. Ed … well, that wasn't his real name. Not that he told me one way or another, mind you. He didn't tell me much, just enough so I knew he was … well, in hiding."

"In hiding? You mean like from the government? Was he a criminal?" My mind raced with the possibilities. Could that be why he encouraged Gin to get a German shepherd? As a criminal, he would know firsthand what would make the best deterrents against being attacked.

She stiffened. "Why do you assume he was a criminal? Maybe he was in the Witness Protection Program?"

"Well, if he was, he still might be a criminal. You hear about that with the mob—some low-level accountant turns against the rest of the organization."

She rolled her eyes. "I doubt that he was low level wherever he was or whatever he was doing. But to answer your question, I have no idea who or what he was hiding from. Nor do I know why. He was careful not to tell me specifics. Said the less I knew, the better."

She hesitated for a moment, biting her bottom lip. "Looking back, I can see there were signs. For instance, after that encounter in the woods, he asked me if I was going to file a police report. I told him absolutely not. I already knew there would be little that the police could do, as the perverts didn't actually do anything to me. So the last thing I was going to do was subject myself to being questioned over and over about it. I thought he was going to try to talk me into it, like Blythe did, but instead, he seemed oddly relieved. I was too traumatized at that time to think much about it. Maybe if I had, it might have given me pause, but maybe not."

"Wait, what are you saying? That Ed *knew* those guys?" *And you don't think he was a criminal?* I wanted to add, but the icy stare she immediately threw at me kept my mouth closed.

"I already told you, I don't know anything. Ed made sure he told me as little as possible. All I know is that shortly after those two were arrested, he told me he was going to have to leave Redemption. When I asked how long he was going to be gone, he said he was never coming back." She bit her lip again and looked down at her lap. "We had just finished our normal dog-training session, and Ed was petting Rex as we talked. I asked him if there was anything he could tell me, but he said no. He'd already said too much, and it was better for both of us if I knew as little as possible. Normally, I would have dropped it then and there, as I'm not someone who likes to pry into other people's business. But Ed …" Her face softened ever so slightly. "We had gotten close over a year's time. I was seeing him at least every week, sometimes twice a week, and, well …" She cleared her throat. "In that moment, I realized I didn't want him to go. I tried to convince him to stay, but…" her voice trailed off at the memory, and she gave her herself a hard shake.

"Anyway, as we talked, Rex began licking his face, and Ed looked so sad that I suddenly realized I couldn't let him go alone. He needed to take Rex with him.

"At first, Ed refused. He said Rex was my dog, and I needed him more than Ed did. The whole point of me getting a dog was for protection, after all. I told Ed I didn't need protection anymore, since the perverts were gone, and I would be fine. Besides, if he took Rex, I could finally get a little dog. That made him laugh." She smiled at the memory, but I could still see the sheen of unwept tears in her eyes.

"It took some time to convince him, but finally, he agreed. There was only one problem—how could he take Rex without raising all sorts of questions? I mean, Blythe knew I went to a weekly dog-training lesson. If I came home with no dog … I couldn't even imagine the questions she would ask. She loved Rex, maybe even more than I did.

"Luckily, I knew she had a doctor's appointment on Friday, and I figured she would be gone for most of the day. I arranged for Ed to come by and take the dog then, and I would tell Blythe, my family, and anyone else who asked that Rex got out of the yard and ran off. It wasn't easy; I got a lot more questions than I thought, not to mention how sad I was to let him go and knowing how much I would miss him." Rocky took that moment to jump into Gin's lap and start licking her face, and she laughed. "It was worth it, though. Rex absolutely adored Ed, and it was the least I could do for Ed after all he did for me." She gave me a sideways look. "I'd do it all over again, too, even knowing I would have to endure you and your meddling ways."

Chapter 18

I opened the gate to let myself and Scout out of the dog park, my head still spinning over what Gin had told me. The fact that my instincts were right, and the disappearance of both Ed and Rex were related, was still blowing my mind. All I wanted to do was tell Aunt Tilde, Mildred, and Nora, but I had promised Gin I wouldn't. Even though I didn't completely buy the story Ed allegedly told Gin. It felt a little too pat for me. He was hiding something, or maybe Gin was the one hiding something … or maybe, they both were. Regardless, something still felt off. And even though I knew it was also still none of my business, it continued to gnaw at me, like a scab that refused to heal. There was something niggling at me, something important about this case, but the more I tried to grasp it, the more it floated tantalizingly out of reach.

Scout suddenly jerked on his leash, nearly pulling my arm out of socket. "Scout, what are you doing?" I yelped as he started dragging me toward the passenger door of a blue car. He jumped up, putting his front legs on the door, and turned to me with a doggy grin.

"Scout, what are you doing? Why are you on this car? You're going to scratch the paint." I looked around desperately, hoping no one was paying any attention, but as far as I could tell, all the women in the dog park were too busy chatting with each other to notice me or Scout. Gin had re-joined her group, and they were all sitting at the picnic table while their dogs romped around them.

Scout jumped down and head butted me. I was about to pull him away when I suddenly realized it was Gin's car.

A lot of groceries. Too many. Especially for a single woman.

Aunt Tilde's voice floated through my head, although I told myself it didn't mean anything. Just because Gin was buying a quantity of food neither Aunt Tilde nor Mildred thought a single woman should be (never mind I still didn't know exactly how they knew what she bought), I still couldn't stop myself from taking a step toward the car.

This is ridiculous, I muttered as I glanced back toward the dog park. Gin seemed to be in a deep conversation with the woman who was still fanning herself. Scout nudged me again with his head. I reached down to rub behind his ears as I peeked into the passenger side window.

The first thing I noticed was that it was messier than I'd expected. There was a leash, a bunch of plastic bags, an open bag of treats, a couple of dog toys …

And what looked like a map scribbled on a half-sheet of paper.

It was on the floor and mostly covered by an empty water bottle, so I couldn't be sure.

I tried the door, figuring it would be locked. Imagine my surprise when it opened.

I quickly bent down, feeling Scout's hot breath against my bare arm, and pulled the piece of paper toward me. It was indeed a map and directions. I studied it, trying to commit it to memory, even as I could feel the heat of the sun beating down on the back of my neck and the sweat dripping down my shirt—even while remaining conscious of the fact that Gin wasn't that far away, and at any moment, could realize I was messing around inside her car. If she thought I wasn't minding my business before …

I couldn't even go there.

There was no final address, just a rough drawing of a circle with what I assumed to be a street name. Once I had committed it to memory, or at least hoped to have committed it to memory, I closed the car door and hurried away to my own car. I didn't dare turn around to see if Gin had seen me. Even when I was safely tucked inside my own car and frantically scribbling my notes down in a notebook I kept in the glove box for … well, maybe not precisely this purpose, but something close to it, I didn't dare look at her. Even though I felt like I was being a child, covering my eyes and inwardly proclaiming, "I can't see you, so you can't see me," I still couldn't bring myself to risk it. It felt better, and safer, to just keep my head down and go.

***

For the second time in a 24-hour period, I sat in my car watching. With Scout once again in the backseat, my eyes were fixed on Gin's house. It was certainly starting to feel like I was on a one-woman stakeout. Or, more precisely, a one-woman and one-dog stakeout.

Yesterday, when I returned from the dog park, the first thing I did was open a map of Redemption to see if I could decipher the directions I'd found in Gin's car. It was an utter failure. I spent nearly an hour pouring over the map, but could find nothing even remotely close.

I finally broke down and asked Aunt Tilde if she had any ideas where the location was. I had come up with a lame story that a friend of mine had found the note, and I was helping her try to decipher it. It was such a ridiculous lie, I could barely choke it out, and I braced myself for the unavoidable onslaught of questions. But she was surprisingly accepting of my story. She said I was probably looking at the outside of Redemption, in the woods near the state park.

"There are a few neighborhoods back there where the homes aren't really identified," Aunt Tilde said. "They look more like trails, and you can't find any numbers on the homes. Some of them are completely off-grid, so there's not even a utility hookup. And it goes without saying that mail isn't being delivered out there. I would guess that's where it is, and why there's no address."

I felt a tingle run up my spine. Homes that are so remote they might even be off the grid? Sounded ideal for someone in hiding. "If that's the case, are there people living there?"

"I think most of them are summer homes, or cabins, although I'm sure there are a few hardy souls who stay out there all year," Aunt Tilde said. She squinted at my crude drawing again. "Based on this, it might be difficult for your friend to precisely pinpoint the exact house. Hopefully, something will stand out to help her figure it out."

Something that would stand out? I had no idea what that might be. If my hunch was right, and Ed was hanging out in one of those unmarked homes, I seriously doubted he would have hung a "Welcome" sign on the porch.

But short of going door to door, how would I possibly know which house was the one Ed was living in? For that matter, how would I even recognize him? It wasn't like there was a photo of him in the newspaper. Unless … how many single older men would just happen to have a German shepherd with them?

And if, rather than focus on looking for a man, I instead tried to find a German shepherd, maybe Scout could help again.

Which was how I found myself watching Gin's house, waiting for her to leave. At least, I was hoping she would. If she didn't, I would have no choice but to come back the next day. And I really, really didn't want to. I could practically hear the ticking of the clock in my head, and every moment I wasted was another one in which he might disappear again. And then, I would never know the truth.

The front door opened. I leaned forward in my seat, holding my breath. Gin emerged, a large tote bag slung over one shoulder and holding a leash with the other hand. Rocky danced around her feet, nearly tripping her. She reached around to slam her front door shut before starting toward the sidewalk, Rocky trotting alongside her.

Oh no. I immediately threw myself backward and scrunched down as far as I could, praying she couldn't see me as I silently cursed myself. How stupid could I be? I had been so fixated on her leaving, it didn't even occur to me she might decide to take Rocky for a walk. And what if she recognized my car? Or recognized Scout, who was still standing on the backseat, peering out the window?

Stupid.

Holding my breath, I watched Gin walk down the driveway and turn in the opposite direction from where I was parked. As the distance grew between us, I wondered if I dared get out of the car. I had no idea how long her walk would last; for all I knew, it would be once around the block, and back in the house, which I knew wouldn't give me enough time.

Ugh. I really should have thought this through.

While I sat there stewing over my options, I watched Gin suddenly cross the street and pick her way up a driveway alongside a couple of cars. I also noticed vehicles parked in front of the street, as well. She rang the doorbell, and after a moment, a woman answered.

She gave Gin a hug, Rocky a pet, and ushered her in, shutting the door firmly behind her.

I stayed where I was for several minutes, watching the door, but I saw no sign of Gin. I did see another car arrive, park in the street, and a woman with a large tote bag similar to Gin's hurry up the driveway. The same woman who let Gin in appeared at the front door, giving the newcomer a hug and ushering her inside, as well.

Maybe this was some sort of club, like a book or knitting club. She did say she was back into knitting again, right? And she was carrying a big tote bag, which might be holding her supplies. And if that were the case, maybe she wouldn't reappear for an hour or so.

I could only hope.

I quickly slid out of the car and hurried up to Blythe's house. Hopefully, Blythe wasn't also at this neighborhood club meeting, or the whole mission was going to be for naught.

I rang Blythe's doorbell, waiting impatiently on the porch. Inside, I could hear the doorbell jangling, and I listened carefully for footsteps or a voice … really, for anything. But all I heard was silence.

Drat. This was what I was afraid of. Gin and Blythe both being gone at the same time. I was going to have no choice but to come back, even though the ticking clock inside me was now as loud as a bong.

I pressed the doorbell again, even though I was sure it was useless. I was just going to have to hope that Gin was also planning on leaving the following day, and Blythe would stay put …

"Hold on, I'm coming." Footsteps creaked toward me, and a minute later, the door opened, and Blythe stood in front of me. She wore a flowered housedress that had what looked like a coffee stain across the front, and she appeared tired and pale, like she hadn't been sleeping well. But she smiled when she saw me. "Emily! What a nice surprise. Sorry, I was in the basement doing laundry. Would you like to come in?"

"Sure," I said, stepping into the foyer. "Although I'm so sorry I can't stay long."

Her face crumpled slightly, and a part of me almost wanted to take it back and spend a half-hour drinking her too-sour lemonade. But I knew there was no way I could sit still for any length of time, and Scout was in the car. Inwardly, I promised myself I would come back very soon for a visit.

"What can I do for you?" She asked as she began tidying an already perfectly straight pile of magazines stacked on a small table next to the door. From what I could see of the house, I was pleasantly surprised to find it immaculate, everything neatly organized and in its place. It even smelled nice, of lemon polish and fresh-cut flowers.

But, alas, I wasn't here for lemonade and a chat in a house after my own heart. I had a job to do. And now that I was standing in front of Blythe, I was thinking the odds of my plan actually working weren't all that high. Of course, if it didn't, I wasn't going to give up, but it would sure make my life more difficult. "I was hoping you could … err … well, get Rex's collar for me. Just for a day or so." It was probably a bridge too far to ask Blythe to steal it, even though that was exactly what I was asking. However, I preferred to think of it as borrowing without permission.

She gave me a puzzled look. "Why do you want Rex's collar?"

I sucked in a deep breath. Here went nothing. "Remember how I told you I worked at a detective agency? Well, there's a lab tech who owes me a favor, and he thought there were some … tests he could do on the collar that might help us pinpoint what happened to Rex."

It was such a boldfaced lie, I couldn't believe I had been able to say it with a straight face. This wasn't me. I prided myself on my honesty. And yet, there I was telling an outlandish fib to a woman so she would steal a dog collar for me (ahem, borrow without permission, for only a day or two). What had I turned into? This was absolutely something that Aunt Tilde would do in a heartbeat, but not me.

Although … I wasn't lying about the results—if she gave me the collar, it very well might help me pinpoint what happened to Rex. Not that I would be able to tell her the truth. But…maybe when all was said and done, I would be able to share something that would bring Blythe some closure. Not the truth, but something.

Her face lit up. "Really? I had no idea there were tests like that."

I swallowed hard. "Well, you know … computers … they can do amazing things with them."

"That's incredible. Of course, I'd be happy to do whatever I can to help. You know how much I would love to know what happened to Rex." Her forehead puckered. "But I'm not sure how Gin would react."

"What if you just … get the collar?" I suggested. "I promise I'll bring it back in a day or so. Do you think she would even miss it?"

Blythe stood quietly for a moment, her forehead still puckered thinking about it, before her face brightened. "I just need a minute."

***

I pulled over to the side of the road and parked. Tall trees surrounded the road, blocking out much of the sun. Rex's collar was on the seat next to me, and Scout's breath was warm on my neck.

I still couldn't believe what I had just done. It was so unlike me on so many levels. Living in Redemption was definitely changing me, and perhaps not for the better.

Well, there was no time to think about that. After all I'd done to get the collar, it would be really stupid to not do anything with it.

I grabbed Scout's leash and Rex's collar. Once we were both out of the car, I showed Scout the collar. "This is Rex's collar. I'm going to let you sniff it, and then, I want you to help me find him. Do you think you can do that?"

Scout looked up at me, and I started feeling awfully silly. Did I really think Scout would understand a word I said? Well, it didn't matter much, as I couldn't think of anything else to do.

Scout, however, sat his butt down and looked at me very seriously, like he *had* understood every word. I doubted that, but I let him sniff the collar anyway. His ears perked up, and he immediately began to lead me down the street. I stuffed the collar into my pocket and followed him.

I had followed the map to the best of my ability, and we ended up on a circular dirt path with a couple of cul de sacs off of it. I drove through it once, and I could see at least a half-dozen cabins from the road. Plus, I imagined there were other homes and cabins tucked further in. Just the cursory look was overwhelming, so if this experiment with Scout didn't work, I didn't know what I was going to do.

Scout, however, seemingly had no qualms as he confidently led me down the road. The air was cool and smelled of pine and dampness. It was also very quiet. Other than the rustling of small animals scurrying away and the chirping of a few birds, there was almost complete silence. No sounds of traffic or lawn mowers or children playing or anything else you generally hear in a neighborhood. Other than Scout, I was completely alone, and no one even knew where I was. If something were to happen to me …

Maybe this wasn't a very smart idea after all.

Just as I was starting to rethink the whole plan, Scout sniffed the air, then turned the corner and led me into one of the cul de sacs. It was just as quiet there as it was on the main road. I looked at the few houses I could see from the road, and they appeared empty. Actually, they looked like they had been vacant for years. There was an air of neglect around them, and I was finding it difficult to imagine anyone ever choosing to stay there.

There was a skittering sound from one of the cabins and a crackling of leaves as a blur of fur burst out of the bushes and came charging toward us. It was huge and fast and full of teeth.

I jerked Scout toward me and tried to back up, my brain trying to piece together what type of animal it was. A coyote? A wolf?

Oh no.

My mind raced, frantically trying to remember what to do when one encountered a wolf. Were you supposed to run down a hill? No, that was a bear … but it didn't matter, because there weren't any hills around anyway. I couldn't climb a tree, but there was no way I could drag Scout up with me. Maybe playing dead would work … or was *that* what you're supposed to do if you encountered a bear?

A shrill whistle pierced the air, and the wolf stopped. Just froze, right at the edge of the lawn. It happened so fast, I could only stare at it, blinking.

And then a couple of things hit me at once.

First, it wasn't a wolf, but a German shepherd.

Second, Scout's tail was wagging triumphantly.

Third, there was a man standing in the yard, his arms folded across his barrel chest and a scowl on his face.

"Who the hell are you?"

Chapter 19

"Um, I'm Emily," I squeaked. The man was HUGE. He had thick legs that looked like tree trunks, and his biceps were muscular and covered with tattoos. "Are you Ed?"

His eyes narrowed at me, and I could see a vein jump in his jaw. "I don't know any Ed. Who are you again, and what are you doing here?"

My gaze fell on the German shepherd, who remained as still as a statue. The dog looked at me, and I swear I heard a faint growl. Oh geez. I tightened my lead on Scout, pulling him closer to me, as sweat started to trickle down my back. The man alone looked like he could pick me up and carry me off with one hand, which was bad enough, but then to have a huge German shepherd as backup? Where was the sweet dog that Blythe kept talking about? This one looked like a killer.

Although it was possible it wasn't Rex, and I just happened to stumble upon another man living out here with a German shepherd. Yeah, right. "I'm a friend of Gin's ..." I began.

I didn't expect his reaction. He suddenly strode toward me, his eyes flashing. "What did you do to Gin?"

"Um," I squeaked again, scurrying back several steps and pulling Scout with me. "Why would I do anything to Gin? I just said she's my friend." Which was a bit of an exaggeration, but in this case, it felt like the smart thing to say, as I didn't want him to get any madder than he already was.

His scowl deepened. Ugh. It didn't work. "You're lying. Gin would never say anything to anyone. What did you do to her?" He clenched his fists, causing his very large muscles to tense up.

Oh boy. I was in trouble. "I used to work for the Duckworths," I blurted out.

It was a gamble, and one I hadn't intended on using, at least until I had a chance to feel him out, but I also didn't think I had any other choice.

He hesitated, and I saw something unreadable flash across his face, but it was gone before I could decipher it. "You used to? As in you don't anymore?"

I swallowed hard as I nodded.

He studied me, his eyes sweeping me up and down. "I think you better come inside." He turned and started heading for the house, whistling for the dog, who immediately popped up and charged after him.

I stared at him, mouth gaping like a fish. That was it? I could still feel the adrenaline racing through my veins as I watched him and the dog disappear through a side door of the cabin. Was I really going to follow him, a complete stranger, into his home?

It was so quiet around me. So still. Not a bird chirped or a squirrel rustled through the leaves. Just me and Scout … and no one knew I was there.

Was I really going to do this?

I knew the answer and cautiously started toward the door. If this really was Ed, and I believed it was, then it was the same man who saved Gin that one fateful day when she was hiking. I found it hard to believe that the same man who had stepped in to save a stranger would attack me.

And quite honestly, if he really wanted to hurt me, he would have. There was no one around, so what difference would it make to go into his house versus staying in the front yard? Not to mention that I was sure he could easily catch me if I had tried to run back to my car, despite being a good twenty to thirty years older than me. And if he didn't feel like chasing after me, he could always send Rex.

But why would I go through all of this trouble to find him if I wasn't going to stick around to hear his side of the story?

As I drew closer to the house, I saw he had left the side door open a crack. I gingerly pushed it open and stepped inside, Scout pressed right up against my leg.

I found myself standing in a combination living room/kitchen. There was a large fireplace at one end and a hallway leading to what

I assumed to be a bedroom at the other end. In front of the fireplace was a broken-down, stained couch with a dog bed next to it. Rex was in the dog bed, his ears perked as he watched me. Ed was in the kitchen area banging around and doing something that I couldn't quite see. There was a small table with two chairs behind him.

"You can have a seat on the couch if you want," he said, not looking at me.

I looked at Rex. He looked at me.

"Don't worry, he's not going to hurt you."

Rex licked his chops.

"I would keep your dog on a leash, though. He's good with other dogs, but better safe than sorry."

I wasn't sure what that meant, but I kept a firm hand on my leash as I slowly made my way to the couch and perched on the edge. Actually, I tried to perch on the edge, but as there was at least one broken spring, and I ended up falling backward.

"Sorry about that," Ed said. He was standing in front of me, and he handed me a glass of what appeared to be soda. "And sorry there's no ice. But it's wet at least. Should help with the heat."

I took the glass, not necessarily because I wanted it, but because I didn't know how to refuse. Although he was right about the temperature. The house was stuffy and hot and smelled like wet dog, mildew, and dirty socks.

He dragged over a kitchen chair and sat in front of me, sipping his drink. "So what happened?"

It took me a minute to realize he was asking me about the Duckworths. "About a month ago, they fired me."

His eyes bored into me from over his glass. "Why?"

"Because I found out something I shouldn't have." I preferred not to get into the whole sordid story, but I would if I had to.

In this case, it didn't seem necessary. Rather than ask me questions, he slowly nodded. "That happens." There was a sadness in his eyes that surprised me, but it was also reassuring … at least a teensy, tiny bit.

"Is that what happened to you, too?" I asked. "You found out something you shouldn't have?"

"In a way." He paused, studying me carefully. "How did you know about me and the Duckworths?"

I ran my finger around the rim of the glass. "I overheard a couple of them talking about Ice going missing. Of course, my first thought was we were out of ice, and I jumped in and said I'd call someone to take care of it. That was my job, you see. Officially, I was the office manager, although unofficially, I was the COO, but regardless, it was my job to make sure the office ran smoothly, including making sure we had ice. They immediately got flustered, told me not to bother and changed the subject. I figured they thought I had enough on my plate, which I appreciated, but it was still my job, so I called the maintenance guy to check out the ice maker. He did and told me there was nothing wrong with it, and there was plenty of ice in the machine. I will admit I thought it was odd, but then I got busy with something else and I just … um …" I felt myself blushing. I had been so naïve back then, so convinced the illusion I was living in was real. Only now was I starting to realize how wrong I had been—that those casual conversations I had overheard, the scribbled notes on my boss's desk, the misfiled papers—all the things that sounded faintly sinister, yet I brushed them off, as I was sure there was a perfectly reasonable explanation for everything. "Anyway, I'm now thinking they meant a person named Ice, and you're that person. Am I right?"

"When did this happen?"

I reached out to pet Scout, who was sitting so close to me, I could feel his warm fur against my legs. "I don't remember the exact date, but it was roughly a year ago." The same time the criminals who attacked Gin were arrested, and the same time Ed disappeared. I knew it was a stretch—even if the Duckworths had been referring to a person named Ice, the idea it could be this man was insane. What were the odds?

And yet, deep in my gut, I knew I was right.

He took another long drink of his soda and sat back in his chair, gazing up at the ceiling. "It was short for Ice Man. I got the nickname because I could do whatever needed to be done … like I had ice in my veins." He glanced back at me, and I was suddenly aware of how pale blue his eyes were, almost like he was *made* of ice. And even though it was so hot in the cabin that beads of sweat were forming on my forehead, I was suddenly cold myself, as the implications of what he just said finally started to sink in.

"You mean you …" I couldn't even finish the sentence. For that matter, I couldn't even think straight. The idea that I was right about Ed and the Duckworths collided with what all that implied—that the Duckworths had someone on their payroll who needed to have ice in his veins for the work that he did for them.

What had I gotten myself into?

"The less you know, the better," he said, cutting me off. "Trust me."

I pressed my lips together and stared down at my soda as a whisper of doubt started to creep into my thoughts. This was crazy. I didn't know this man at all. He was a complete stranger to me. All I knew was he supposedly disappeared a year ago with someone else's dog. He could be yanking my chain as he agreed with me, pretending he was involved with the Duckworths, and I would have no way to prove or disapprove it.

Meanwhile, I knew the Duckworths. I had worked for them. They were businesspeople. They owned a lot of businesses in this state. Legal businesses. Completely above board. This wasn't the mob we were talking about. There was no reason for a legal business to have someone with the nickname Ice Man on their payroll. I should stand up, hand him my soda, walk back to my car, and put this entirely out of my mind.

But, deep down, in my bones, I believed him. I knew he was telling me the truth. And it made me ill to think I had worked for them for so many years.

He must have seen something in my face, because I could hear him let out a deep sigh. "Although … I didn't work for the Duckworths."

My head shot up. "What? But you just said …"

"I knew who they were," he cut in. "They were … well, I guess you could say they were in a similar line of work as the company I worked for. I wouldn't call them rivals, exactly … maybe a cross between associates and competitors. So, when I decided I needed to leave, I knew I had to find somewhere to disappear. And I knew my company pretty much stayed out of Wisconsin, as it made things … less complicated. So that's why I settled in Redemption."

"But you're less than an hour away from Riverview, which is where the Duckworths' headquarters are," I said. "Wouldn't you want to be further away?"

He gave me a look. "Do you understand this town's history? There's a reason why the Duckworths, for the most part, leave Redemption alone. There's a lot of strange and unexplained events going on here that even ruthless organizations want no part of."

I had to admit, there was something to that.

"Anyway, at first, I didn't have any issues. I was able to settle in without any trouble, with my new name and identity, and all was going well. Until the day I met Gin on that trail." Something flitted across his expression, disappearing so fast, I could almost believe I hadn't seen anything.

But only almost. Because I had seen the same yearning on Gin's face. And it made me both happy and sad—happy because I now knew Gin's feelings were reciprocated, but sad because they couldn't be together.

He straightened up, running a hand over his bald head. "Anyway, if you talked to Gin, you already know that part of the story. The smart thing would have been to have walked away and not blown my cover. But …" he shot me a rueful smile. "I was never known for my smarts."

"So you did know the guys who were harassing Gin?" It was half question, half statement.

His smile turned predatory. "No, but by the time I was done with them, they would have realized they weren't dealing with just anyone. They would have known I had … specialized training." His smile faded. "It was dumb. In retrospect, I should have handled it better. More discreetly. But I wanted to make sure they knew to leave Gin alone. And I wanted it done fast, so I could catch up to her." He lips twisted, like he was disgusted with himself. "At the time, I told myself it didn't matter. They were just a couple of punks, and not very smart ones. I figured they would put the whole sorry episode out of their minds and not ask around. Living in Redemption had made me sloppy. I had been under the radar for so long, I think I assumed I was safe. But of course, in my line of work, you're never safe. I, of all people, should have remembered that."

"I don't understand. They figured out who you were?" I asked.

"No, I wouldn't go that far, but they figured out enough to know that the Duckworths would be very interested to know about the encounter."

"Why would they be interested if you didn't work for them?"

He looked up at the ceiling, frowning a little, as if trying to figure out how to explain without telling me much of anything. "Let's just say this: I was good at what I did. Very good. So good, I had a built up enough of a reputation so it wasn't just my company who knew who I was, but also other … associates in other companies, like the Duckworths. And everything was … well, I don't know if 'fine' is exactly the right word. Maybe 'running smoothly' is more accurate. That is, until the day I realized I couldn't do that work anymore. I was done. And I walked away.

"But you don't get to just walk away from that type of work. You just don't. So, I knew I was going to have to disappear, which I did. I spent a few years moving from place to place, staying under the radar, until I settled in Redemption. I never intended to stay for as long as I did, but …" he shrugged. "You know what people say who live here. Redemption, the town, decides who lives here and who doesn't. I always thought it was nonsense, yet I still stayed. Even though I should have known better."

"It is nonsense," I said forcefully. Maybe a little too forcefully. Because how could a town decide who stayed and who left? Of course, how could a small town have so many disappearances and other unexplained events either, but that was probably just dumb luck. Neither thing had anything to do with the adults disappearing in 1888. It was all a bunch of superstition. Besides, there was no way Redemption was going to decide when it was time for me to leave.

He glanced at me, his eyes lidded, but otherwise didn't respond to my outburst. "It wasn't until those punks got arrested that I started to get an uneasy feeling that I had compromised myself. I was able to get in touch with a friend on the inside, who confirmed my suspicions. So, I knew I was going to have to leave, and fast. My plan was to leave immediately after my lesson with Gin. I wasn't going to tell her, but … well …" He sighed. "I have definitely made a number of poor choices."

"But why would the Duckworths care that you're living here?" I asked. "You weren't bothering anyone, and you had nothing to do with them, right?"

He gave me an unreadable look. "I told you, I have a reputation."

"Yes, but …"

He was still staring at me, and suddenly, the answer clicked into place. "They were going to tell your old company where you were."

He ran his hands over his face. "The Duckworths aren't stupid. They knew my old company would owe them a favor if they found me for them."

What kind of favor? It was on the tip of my tongue to ask, but I decided I didn't want to know the answer. Again, I saw myself working in their office, the break room always stocked with coffee and water and snacks, all bought by the company. The generous bonuses they paid. My company car.

But it was more than that. I had truly loved my job. And the Duckworths did so much good, including donating incredible amounts of money through the Duckworth Foundation. I had always believed that by helping their business be more successful, I was contributing to all the good they were doing in the state. Except now, I had to question whether they were doing any good at all. Or was it all part of the illusion?

"You should go now." His voice was quiet, his gaze steady. "Forget about this. Forget about me. And definitely forget about the Duckworths." He shot me a small smile that didn't reach his eyes. "I know it doesn't feel like it, but they did you a favor by firing you. You should stay as far away as possible from them."

At this point, I wasn't sure about anything except for one thing—I definitely needed to get out of there. I struggled to stand up, trying not to spill my soda or flip backward onto the broken couch again. In a flash, he was there, taking my drink and helping me up. "Sorry again. I should have given you the chair." Even though he sounded sincere, looking into those pale-blue eyes, I didn't think he was. I had a feeling he'd done it on purpose, probably because he didn't want me to get too comfortable, so I would leave faster.

"There's just one more thing," I said. His eyes narrowed, so I hurried on before he could throw me out. "Why are you even back here? If your cover has been blown, that is."

He looked away. "I had some unfinished business I had to attend to."

I pictured the map in Gin's car, and I wondered she was the "unfinished business," or if there was more. But seeing the tightness in his jaw, I knew I would never know the answer to that.

"And now I have a question for you." He turned back to me, his eyes sharp. "How did you find me?"

Well, two could play this game. "I had a little help," I said, nudging Scout.

He raised an eyebrow, folding an arm across his chest. "You're trying to tell me the dog found me?"

I shrugged. "He has a really good nose." Rex's collar was heavy in my pocket, but I had a feeling it would be the wrong move to show him.

He rolled his eyes.

"Maybe it was a lucky guess," I said.

He gave me a pointed stare. "I'm serious. Did Gin …" he stopped, his throat working, and suddenly, I understood.

"It wasn't Gin," I said quickly. "I had … well, I did some poking around on my own." I could feel my face turning red. "I found the article in the newspaper about you disappearing, and I talked to the neighbor. I sort of put two and two together."

He briefly closed his eyes, but not before I saw the relief in them. I told myself I had made the right decision, and besides, I wasn't really lying. Not exactly. Gin hadn't told me where he was. I had found the map because I had been poking around in her car.

Just like you didn't steal a collar. You're only temporarily borrowing it, a voice inside me said, and I shoved it away. I didn't have time to deal with that now.

Chapter 20

"There you are," Aunt Tilde sang out as Scout and I walked through the door of the Redemption Detective Agency. Mildred and Nora were also there, along with Smoke and Sherlock. "Thanks to you, the case is now solved!"

I stared at her as a ball of dread filled my stomach. They couldn't possibly know about Ed, right? How could they? I hadn't said a word, and I was sure Ed didn't say anything to anyone, so unless Scout had learned to talk …

As if on cue, Scout looked up at me, his tail thumping the floor and an innocent expression on his doggy face. I petted him behind his ears, and he moseyed off to lay in his bed. Smoke took one look at him and immediately flattened his ears as he headed for the other side of the room.

Earlier that morning, I had swung by Blythe's house to return the collar and give her an update on Rex. I told her it appeared Gin gave Rex to a very nice family who really needed a guard dog. "I can't share any details; it's too dangerous for them. Just know that Rex is safe, happy, and well cared for."

It wasn't that far from the truth, but hopefully far enough that no one could possibly link it to Ed. Besides, Blythe had been so relieved to hear that Rex was okay that I knew in my gut I was doing the right thing. I told Blythe I wasn't sure how Gin found out about the family, but it seemed Rex's original owner had something to do with it. Gin knew it was the right thing to do, and because she didn't want anyone trying to find Rex, thereby endangering the family, she made up the story about Rex running away.

"That makes so much sense," Blythe said, nodding. She promised me she wouldn't tell a soul, nor would she ever bring it up to Gin.

"It will be our secret," I told her, which made her beam. I really thought she would keep it to herself, but if Aunt Tilde knew …

She must have seen something in my blank expression because she kept talking. "Jan's case!"

"Oh, Jan! Of course." I had been so focused on Rex and Gin, I had managed to completely forget about Jan and her husband. "So, you were able to get photos of him cheating?"

"That's the thing. He wasn't cheating," Aunt Tilde said.

Mildred gave her a sour look. "Not while we were watching, anyway."

Nora gave her a sharp look. "You shouldn't say that about our client."

I blinked at her. "Client?"

Nora flashed me a broad smile. "Yes! As it turned out, he was also in the market for a private investigator, so it was a good thing I gave him my card."

"Just as you always say, 'There's no such thing as bad PR,'" Aunt Tilde said.

"Um … I don't think I'm the one who said that," I said.

"Oh, you're being modest again," Aunt Tilde said, waving her hand. "You need to learn how to own your brilliance. I've got the perfect self-help book for you. It's all the rage, you know. Remind me to give it to you."

I absolutely was not going to remind her of that. I could only imagine what drivel she had in mind to hand me. Besides, I was still trying to get my head around the new case we were talking about. "You're saying the guy who tripped over Smoke hired us?"

"He did," Nora said cheerfully.

"But isn't he allergic to cats?" I asked.

"That's why we had to meet him at Aunt May's Diner," Nora said, her forehead puckering. "It was too bad, too. Smoke would have liked to see him again." She sighed, before turning to Mildred. "I told you he was good for business. It was a good thing he was on that stakeout with us. He should be our mascot."

If anything, Mildred's expression became even more sour.

"What did Jan's husband hire us to do?" I asked.

"Find out if Jan was cheating on him," Aunt Tilde said.

My jaw dropped. "Wait. You're telling me that both Jan and her husband are our clients? And they each hired us to spy on the other?"

"Yep," Nora grinned.

"And did you tell them both that we're representing them both?" I asked, unsure if I even wanted to hear the answer.

"Of course not," Aunt Tilde sniffed. "How could that have worked out, if they knew they were being watched?"

I closed my eyes. "That can't be legal." Mentally, I added it to my list of pending research topics.

Aunt Tilde flapped her hands. "I'm sure it's legal *enough*. The state can't keep clients from hiring us."

"They certainly can, if there's a conflict of interest," I said.

"What conflict?" Nora asked. "We work on their cases separately. It's not like we'll be watching them both at the same time."

"I still say the husband was cheating on her," Mildred broke in. "And if it hadn't been for Smoke, we would have found the proof."

"If it hadn't been for Smoke, we never would have discovered the truth," Nora said tartly.

"What truth?" I asked, even as I wondered if any of the three were even capable of finding the actual truth.

"The truth is that *she* was the one cheating on *him*," Nora said triumphantly.

I stared at the three of them. "Really? She's the cheater?"

Mildred grimaced. "As it turns out, Jan was the one who wanted a divorce. But if she left him, and especially if he discovered her … affair, she was afraid she wouldn't get anything in the divorce settlement. But if she could prove he was the one who wasn't being faithful, then she could take him to the cleaners."

I frowned. "But if he wasn't cheating on her, how was she going to prove it?"

Mildred seemed to shrink in her seat. "I guess she was hoping we would … find something that looked … incriminating."

I kept my expression neutral, even as my mind raced. Was that why she hired us, a brand-new detective agency full of brand-new detectives? She was hoping we would give her something that she could spin as proof of cheating, even if there wasn't anything to prove?

"As it turned out, you were right again," Aunt Tilde said. "There *was* something fishy about Jan after all."

As gratifying as it was to know I was right, it didn't outweigh my new concern about being sued, fined, or worse. "Does Jan know you know?"

Aunt Tilde shrugged. "I have no idea."

"You didn't tell her?"

She spread her hands out. "Why would we tell her? She didn't hire us to investigate her infidelity."

"We gave her the good news that her husband was faithful," Nora said before thoughtfully chewing on her bottom lip. "Although she didn't seem to think it was good news."

"We don't know for sure her husband was faithful," Mildred corrected her. "We just weren't able to find any evidence he wasn't."

"True, but I think we're missing the bigger picture," Aunt Tilde said. "We cracked not one case, but two. We're on a roll!"

"Yes!" Nora did a little dance. "Go team! We're solving the unsolvable."

I tried not to wince. Yet another thing that could land us in hot water.

"What about you, Emily?" Aunt Tilde asked. "Were you able to discover what happened to that dog?"

That perked Mildred up. "Oh yes. And who was buried in the backyard?"

"No one is buried in Gin's backyard," I said quickly.

"How do you know?" Mildred asked. "Did you investigate?"

"Actually, I did." I looked Mildred straight in the eyes. "That's why I know you were right."

Mildred's jaw went slack. "I am?" Then, she quickly straightened up. "I mean, of course I am. What am I right about?"

"Trisha. She got so upset because she did used to get confused. Exactly what you told us."

That wasn't exactly what Mildred said, but it was close enough for Mildred to nod knowingly. "Oh yes. I remember that as clearly as yesterday."

"So ... what are you saying? That Gin didn't have a dog after all?" Aunt Tilde asked.

"No, she did. But she's a very private person and didn't want to talk about it anymore," I said. "I'm not sure what happened between them, but I think Trisha was afraid she messed something up for Gin."

"Oh, that makes sense. Trisha was always a sweet girl," Mildred said. "Not the brightest, but definitely one of the most caring."

I didn't think that was exactly true, but it didn't matter. I'd achieved what I'd set out to do. The case of the missing dog (and dog walker) was closed, and no one was the wiser to the truth. Ed's secret was safe. And that was all that mattered.

I'm serious. Watch your back. Especially when it comes to the Duckworths.

Despite myself, I shivered. Yet again, Ed's final words to me as I left his house echoed in my mind. I was trying hard to put it behind me. *Ed's wrong*, I told myself again. *Besides, I was nothing to the Duckworths. They aren't going to do anything to me. That chapter of my life is over.*

But then, I would remember the hardness in Ed's eyes, the intensity of his stare. Telling me to watch my back. That the sheer fact that I knew something embarrassing to the Duckworths was enough to walk around for the rest of my life with a target on my back.

No. That was nonsense. I didn't know why the Duckworths knew Ed's nickname (and maybe they didn't … maybe it was just a massive coincidence that they happened to be talking about ice when Ed disappeared), but it didn't have anything to do with me. I had moved on. They had moved on. And maybe, eventually, after a few more years, I could get another job as a COO for a Riverview-based business.

They couldn't blackball me forever. Right?

The tinkling of the bell broke into my thoughts, and I turned to see Nick striding in.

"Nick," Aunt Tilde said, a big smile spreading across her face. "How nice to see you. What can we do for you?"

"I won't be long," he said, locking his eyes with mine. "I was on my way to an appointment, and as you're on the way, I thought I'd stop in to see if my suggestion worked."

"Suggestion? What suggestion?" Mildred asked, her voice suspicious.

Nick's lips twitched. I could feel my cheeks warm.

"A dog park for Scout," I said. "And yes, it was a great suggestion. Exactly what I was looking for."

Nick flashed me one of his cocky grins. "Glad to be of service."

"Emily, you didn't have to ask him," Mildred said. "I would have been happy to have helped you find a dog park."

I couldn't tear my eyes away from Nick's, even though I knew I should. Nick was with Trisha. I had no business drowning in his gaze. "Um …"

"It was really no trouble," Nick said smoothly. "But if you have a moment, I have something I want to …"

He was interrupted by the bell on the door tinkling and a huge bouquet of flowers walking into the agency. "Delivery for Emily," the bouquet said.

Wait, what? Talking flowers? Confused, I looked around the bouquet to find the source of the voice.

"Emily! How beautiful," Mildred said, squeezing my arm. "Who could have sent them?"

"Maybe you have a secret admirer," Nora said.

Who indeed? I took a peek at Nick, but he looked as surprised as the rest of us. Actually, maybe surprised wasn't the right word. He seemed almost … angry.

But why would he be angry? That didn't make sense. Just like it didn't make sense for him to send me flowers, as we weren't dating.

But who else would? Not Jerome. I hadn't returned a single call of his since the disastrous date night. I still hadn't figured out what to do about him, not to mention I had been so distracted trying to find Ed and Rex.

"There's a card," Mildred said as the delivery guy thrust a clipboard into my hand to sign. I barely looked at it as I scribbled my name. "Here," she handed it to me as the man left, accompanied by the tinkling of the bell.

I opened the card. It was from Jerome.

I'm sorry. I was out of line the other night. Of course you should investigate if you have questions, and I should have been more supportive. Can we have dinner and talk about it?

"Oh, it's Jerome," Mildred said, peering over my shoulder. "How sweet. Did you two have a little tiff or something?"

I snatched the card away so she couldn't read it. "Everything is fine. There's no problem. At all. I just need to call him."

Mildred gave me a knowing smile as I headed to the phone, my thoughts in a jumble. Jerome was apologizing to me. I couldn't even remember the last time a man had apologized to me and sent me flowers. Geoff certainly never did that. I was already feeling bad about not returning his calls. Maybe he was right, and I was a little too involved in that case.

I was reaching for the phone, already looking forward to seeing Jerome, when I remembered that Nick had been about to ask me something. I looked around to find him, but he was gone.

A Word From Michele

Want more Emily, Nick and the gang? Keep going with Book 3, *The Mysterious Case of the Missing Ghost*.

Emily Hildebrandt is starting to settle into some of the very strange cases that come through The Redemption Detective Agency's door. Like Aunt Tilde's friend Ruth who claims she's lost a ghost. But how does one lose a ghost?

Grab your copy right here:

mpwnovels.com/r/q/bdwalkghostwide

The Redemption Detective Agency is a spin-off from the *The Charlie Kingsley Mysteries*. If you want to see where it all began, take a look at *The Murder Before Christmas*.

***

You can also check out exclusive bonus content for *The Redemption Detective Agency* here.

The bonus content reveals hints, clues, and sneak peeks you won't get just by reading the books, so you'll definitely want to check it out. You're going to discover a side of Redemption that is only available here.

MPWnovels.com/r/q/redemption-agency-bonus

***

If you enjoyed *The Mysterious Case of the Missing Dog Walker*, it would be wonderful if you would take a few minutes to leave a review and rating on Goodreads:
goodreads.com/book/show/234060632-the-mysterious-case-of-the-missing-dog-walker
or Bookbub:
bookbub.com/books/5282107
(Feel free to follow me on any of those platforms as well.) I thank you and other readers will thank you (as your reviews will help other readers find my books.)

All my series are interconnected and related, and if you'd like to learn more about them, take a look at my website MPWNovels. com. You'll also discover lots of other fun things such as short stories, deleted scenes, giveaways, recipes, puzzles and more.

I've also included a sneak peek of *The Murder Before Christmas* if you'd like to check it out. Just turn the page to get started.

The Mysterious Case of the Missing Ghost
Chapter 1

"My husband is missing. Can you find him?"

I straightened up, pressing the phone tighter against my ear. The voice was frail and thin, and I wondered if I had heard her correctly. "Did you say your husband is *missing*?"

"Yes. I need help finding him. Can you do that?"

"Is this an emergency? Have you tried calling the police?"

"Oh, the police," the voice scoffed. "They can't do anything."

That probably meant it wasn't an emergency, which also indicated her husband had either left on his own accord, or something else had happened to him—something unrelated to foul play. It wasn't against the law for an adult to disappear, so unless there was evidence that he had been taken against his will, the police likely wouldn't get involved. I suspected most of the time, in most other places, there wasn't much in the way of a "something else" option … but this was Redemption, Wisconsin, after all. Here, disappearances were far higher than the national average.

I reached for a pen and yellow pad of paper. "When was the last time you saw him?"

There was a pause. "Well, it's been years since I've seen him."

My pen hovered over the pad. "Years?"

"Oooh, I think Emily has a new client on the phone," Aunt Tilde said, elbowing Mildred. They had been fiddling with the coffee maker all morning, but I was unclear as to whether there was actually a problem with the equipment, or if they were just too busy talking to make any coffee. I waved at her to be quiet.

"Well, my eyes, you know. They're not what they used to be." She sounded apologetic, and I immediately felt bad. This poor woman probably had cataracts, or had maybe even gone blind, and my first thought was that her husband had been missing for a decade, and she was only now getting around to calling someone about it. "But I know he was here two days ago."

"So he's been missing for two days?"

"I think so." There was a hitch in her voice. "I'm worried about him."

"Of course you are, Mrs. …"

"It's Jonasburg, but you can call me Ruth."

I wrote her name down on the yellow pad. "Ruth, then. Can you tell me a little bit about the circumstances surrounding his disappearance? Maybe start with before he left …"

I could hear her swallow. "That's just it. We had a … well, maybe not a *fight*, but definitely a disagreement, and … oh … I don't know what I'll do, if that really was my last interaction with him."

"Let's not think about that now," I said quickly. "Why don't we set up a time to discuss your situation in more detail? Would you be able to come to the office?"

"Oh dear, I'm really not good with driving anymore. Do you think you could come to the house?"

"Sure," I said, quickly jotting down her address as she rattled it off. We agreed to meet later that afternoon, and I hung up the phone.

Both Mildred and Aunt Tilde were watching me closely. "So, tell us about our new client," Aunt Tilde said excitedly.

A nurse who got bored during her retirement and decided it would be fun to open a detective agency with absolutely zero training or experience, Aunt Tilde definitely danced to the beat of her own drum. Today, she was dressed in bright pinks and purples, which didn't clash as much as you might think with her bright-orange hair and matching glasses.

"It's about time we got one," Mildred chimed in, giving me a stern look over her glasses, as though our lack of clients was somehow my fault. Mildred was a retired teacher who jumped at the chance to join her old friend in her newest venture. She dressed far more conservatively than my aunt, though, in pressed pantsuits. She also had her hair done twice a week and wore a little too much perfume. Today, she was dressed in a pale-green pantsuit accented by a single strand of pearls.

"She's not an official client yet," I said. "She wants to see if we can help her find her husband."

Mildred perked up. "Another cheating husband case. Hopefully, we can redeem ourselves with this one."

"Her husband is missing," I said. "That doesn't mean he's cheating."

Mildred waved her hand. "Of course it does. What other explanation would there be?"

"We shouldn't assume he's cheating," Aunt Tilde said. "That's why we investigate."

Mildred raised a nicely shaped eyebrow. "Okay, why do *you* think he's missing, then?"

Aunt Tilde shrugged. "Maybe he got lost."

"What, like he went to the store for cigarettes and never came home?"

"It's possible," Aunt Tilde insisted before letting out a sigh and relenting. "Okay, you're probably right. He's cheating on her."

"Maybe we should hear the entire story before we make assumptions," I suggested.

"I agree. We should get all the details, so we can catch him in the act," Mildred said before flattening her lips, which were covered in bright-pink lipstick, in disapproval. "We don't want to screw it up this time."

"I don't think this case is going to be like Jan's," I said.

"How do you know?" Mildred asked.

"Well, for one, we're looking for a missing husband, not for proof that her husband is cheating on her," I said.

Mildred waved her hand again. "I told you … same thing."

Great. At this rate, I was going to have to find some excuse to keep Mildred from attending the initial meeting. I could already picture her browbeating poor Ruth and insisting her husband had run off with the grocery clerk.

"When is the meeting?" Aunt Tilde asked, as if reading my mind.

Ugh. "This afternoon." I gave Mildred a hard look. "If you come, you can't tell her that her husband is cheating on her. She's very upset. They had a fight before he disappeared."

Mildred looked miffed. "Emily, of course I wouldn't say it. You know me better than that."

Yes, yes, I do know you, and that's why I'm telling you not to. I bit down on my tongue to keep the words from coming out and forced a smile instead. "I just wanted you to know what I know before the meeting. That way, we're all on the same page."

"Good, we should be," Mildred said briskly. "When the time is right, we can tell her the truth about her husband. Not a minute before."

I sighed.

***

"Here we are," I said, gesturing toward a dark-brown split-level house with white trim. Aunt Tilde was driving her signature pink Cadillac with Mildred next to her and me in the backseat.

Aunt Tilde's brows knit together as she leaned over to look through the passenger window. "Isn't this Ruth's house?"

"Yeah, you know her?"

Aunt Tilde twisted her head around to look at me. "Ruth's husband is missing?"

"Yeah." I suddenly felt a chill. "Why? What's wrong? Is her husband sick or something?"

"You could say that," Mildred said.

"What does that mean?" I asked.

Aunt Tilde parked the car by the curb and shot Mildred an unreadable look. "It means it's time to meet our new client." She unbuckled her seatbelt, got out of the car, and started walking determinedly up the driveway. Much to my surprise, Mildred meekly followed without saying a word. I was so taken aback, I sat there for a moment before realizing that at the rate they were going, they would likely start the meeting without me, so I hurriedly got out as well and trotted toward them to catch up.

Aunt Tilde reached the door first, but before she could ring the bell, Ruth opened the door. "Oh Tilde, I'm so glad you're here," she said, her face a wreath of smiles. She looked older than Aunt Tilde, and Mildred for that matter, but I knew that didn't mean she actually was. Her clothes were clean and pressed but faded—a pink and yellow flowered blouse with pink pants—and her gray hair was like dandelion puffs around her head. She wore no makeup, other than bright-pink lipstick, and thick, black-framed glasses.

Aunt Tilde leaned in to give her a half-hug. "Ruth, it's so nice to see you! I'm sorry I haven't been by to visit recently."

"Oh, nonsense," Ruth said, giving Tilde's arm a gentle swat. "Heavens, you've been busy! You've started a detective agency!"

"Well, yes, but I couldn't have done it without my niece, Emily," Aunt Tilde said, gesturing toward me.

"Of course," Ruth said, her sharp eyes giving me a once-over. Something niggled at the back of my head about that, but I couldn't quite put my finger on it. "It's lovely to meet you," Ruth continued, reaching for my hand. She squeezed it, and I could feel her paper-dry skin. "It's wonderful when you can work with your family, isn't it?"

"It's been one of the best parts of opening the agency," Aunt Tilde said, giving me a warm smile that I felt deep in my chest.

Ruth let go of my hand and turned to Mildred. "And Mildred, it's so wonderful to see you, as well. Are you part of the agency too?"

"You better believe it," Mildred said. "I'm the best detective they have."

I tried not to roll my eyes.

"Come in, come in," Ruth said, stepping back from the door so we could enter. The entryway opened onto a large living room to the right with a set of stairs to the left. Further down the hallway, I could see what appeared to be a kitchen. The house was tidy, but not overly so. There was a stack of mail on the coffee table in the living room and a thin layer of dust on the mirror in the hallway. The house smelled of coffee, cinnamon, and an overly aggressive floral air freshener. It was also warm and humid, like she hadn't used an air conditioner in a while. Not that I completely minded; most of the time, people cranked the air conditioning up too high for my liking, but this house felt pretty stuffy. "Would you like something to drink?"

"Oh, we don't want to cause you any trouble," Aunt Tilde said.

Ruth waved her hand. "No trouble. I have a pot of coffee I just finished brewing. I'll bring you all a cup, if you want to have a seat in the living room."

"Coffee sounds lovely, thank you," Aunt Tilde said as we made our way toward the stiff couch, loveseat, and chair ensemble in beige and blue plaid. I sat down on the chair, pulling out my notebook and pen, while Aunt Tilde and Mildred took the couch. Ruth followed a few minutes later, carrying a tray with the coffeepot, four mugs, cream, sugar, and a plate of what looked like homemade cookies. She pushed the pile of mail aside and a couple of envelopes tipped onto the floor. Aunt Tilde scooped them up as Ruth passed coffee in delicate white and gold china cups with matching saucers. I smiled as I accepted mine, even though it meant balancing my coffee on one knee and my notebook on the other.

"So, tell us about Hank," Aunt Tilde said as she doctored her coffee with cream and sugar.

Ruth's hand trembled, causing her cup to clink against her saucer, and she put it down. "It's dreadful. I'm so worried. I think he's really gone."

Aunt Tilde leaned over to put a hand on Ruth's knee. "Of course Hank isn't gone. He loved you too much. He'll always be here."

"I'm sure he's still watching over you," Mildred said, although it sounded like she was choking on the words.

Loved? As in past tense? Watching over you? This didn't sound like a missing husband. It sounded like a deceased husband. But if he was deceased, why did she say he was missing? Did she have dementia? Is that why Mildred looked so miserable? But if she had dementia, how could she be living alone in such a big house?

I studied Ruth, watching her as she dabbed delicately at her eyes, trying to see if there were any signs of dementia, and just like that, the thing that had been niggling at me since we stepped into Ruth's house suddenly popped into my brain.

Ruth wasn't blind. Yes, her glasses looked pretty thick, but she had no trouble pouring coffee into tiny, delicate china cups and passing them around. So, if she hadn't physically seen her husband in years, that probably meant her husband had been dead for years, and if that were the case, then what were we doing here?

"I'm sorry," I broke in, and all three women swung their heads around to look at me. "But is your husband ... did he pass away?"

"Yes, it's been ten years now," Ruth said.

I blinked. Ten *years?* "Oh ... um ... I'm so sorry to hear that. Did you ... remarry?"

"Oh no." Ruth pressed her hand to her heart. "Hank was my one and only. No one could ever replace him."

"He was one-of-a-kind," Aunt Tilde agreed. Next to her, Mildred nodded.

I stared at the three women as I replayed my conversation with Ruth back in my head. No, I was sure she said her husband was missing. But how could he be missing? Unless ... I swallowed hard. *Oh no. Please don't say his ashes. Or, even worse, his body.*

"I'm so sorry, but I'm a little confused," I said. "I thought we were here because you said your husband is missing."

Ruth bobbed her head up and down. "Indeed. He is missing. He disappeared two days ago, and I haven't seen him-well ... *heard* from him, since."

I eyed Aunt Tilde and Mildred, but neither of them looked like this was surprising news to them. Nor did they look particularly alarmed that it appeared their friend was operating under a severe delusion.

Apparently, it was all up to me. "I'm sorry, but exactly what disappeared? Your husband's … ashes?" At the last minute, I found myself unable to say the word "body." Or "corpse."

Ruth burst out laughing. Aunt Tilde joined her, but Mildred was surprisingly silent. "Oh no," Ruth said, when she could finally talk. "Of course not. You poor thing. You thought I was talking to my husband's dead body. No wonder you look so confused."

Relieved, I started smiling as well, even while acknowledging Mildred's lack thereof. It must be something harmless, I decided. Maybe she had a pet with the name "Husband," although the idea of embarking on another missing-dog case gave me the chills. "So who were you talking about?"

"His ghost, dear," Ruth said. "What else would I be talking about?"

Want to keep reading? Grab your copy of *The Mysterious Case of the Missing Ghost* here:

MPWNovels.com/r/bdwalkghostwide

Books and series by Michele Pariza Wacek

Redemption Detective Agency
(Cozy Mysteries)
A spin-off from the Charlie Kingsley series.
https://MPWNovels.com/r/da_dwalker

Charlie Kingsley Mysteries
(Cozy Mysteries)
See all of Charlie's adventures here.
https://MPWnovels.com/r/ck_dwalker

Secrets of Redemption series
(Pychological Thrillers)
The flagship series that started it all.
https://MPWnovels.com/r/rd_dwalker

Mysteries of Redemption
(Psychological Thrillers)
A spin-off from the Secrets of Redemption series.
https://MPWnovels.com/r/mr_dwalker

Riverview Mysteries
(standalone Pychological Thrillers)
*These stories take place in Riverview, which is near
Redemption.*
https://MPWnovels.com/r/rm_dwalker

Access your free exclusive bonus scenes from *The Mysterious Case
of the Missing Dog Walker* right here:
MPWnovels.com/r/q/redemption-agency-bonus/

Acknowledgements

It's a team effort to birth a book, and I'd like to take a moment to thank everyone who helped, especially my wonderful editor, Megan Yakovich, who is always so patient with me, and my husband Paul, for his love and support during this sometimes-painful birthing process.

Any mistakes are mine and mine alone.

About Michele

A USA Today Bestselling, award-winning author, Michele taught herself to read at 3 years old because she wanted to write stories so badly. It took some time (and some detours) but she does spend much of her time writing stories now. Mystery stories, to be exact. They're clean and twisty, and range from psychological thrillers to cozies, with a dash of romance and supernatural thrown into the mix. If that wasn't enough, she posts lots of fun things on her blog, including short stories, puzzles, recipes and more, at MPWNovels.com.

Michele grew up in Wisconsin, (hence why all her books take place there), and still visits regularly, but she herself escaped the cold and now lives in the mountains of Prescott, Arizona with her husband and southern squirrel hunter Cassie.

When she's not writing, she's usually reading, hanging out with her dog, or watching the Food Network and imagining she's an awesome cook. (Spoiler alert, she's not. Luckily for the whole family, Mr. PW is in charge of the cooking.)